BALLSY

BREAKERS HOCKEY #4

ELISE FABER

BALLSY
BY ELISE FABER
Newsletter sign-up

BALLSY

Print ISBN-13: 978-1-63749-046-4
Ebook ISBN-13: 978-1-63749-045-7

BREAKERS HOCKEY SERIES

<u>Broken</u>
<u>Boldly</u>
<u>Breathless</u>
<u>Ballsy</u>
<u>Bewitched</u>
Blowout
Breathe
A Breakers Christmas
Blazed
Bound

ONE

Smitty

I'D FOUND HER.

One look, and I'd known.

Quiet where I was loud. Smart when I wasn't.

Pretty...well, I'd never been and would never be considered pretty.

She was walking down the halls of the practice facility, earbuds in, eyes on the tablet in front of her, totally oblivious to anything except what she was concentrating on.

Certainly, she was oblivious that she was...*mine.*

But I'd known.

Just like Pru had said.

I'd seen the slender column of her throat, the narrow shoulders, and long, long legs, and my heart had kicked.

Hard.

Hard enough that even a big brute like me had paid attention.

Stopped me dead in my tracks, sweat dripping down my spine, my temples, my beard.

And she?

She'd walked by without noticing me. *Me.* A man of my size didn't get missed. *Everyone* knew that I was there. Because if my size didn't get their attention, then certainly my voice would.

But...I hadn't spoken when she'd walked by.

Because of that heart kicking, and I'd also had some lung squeezing action happening. Which meant that any hope of talking to her—*her!*—had disappeared.

I'd been reduced to emitting nothing more than a quiet sort of gurgling sound, and that had, luckily, been missed by *her* because of the earbuds she'd been wearing.

And now, still sweating, I was following her.

Trying to think of something charming and witty that would get her to realize that I was hers, and then we'd have our happy ending, and everything would be fucking cool.

Like Pru and Marcel.

Like Hazel and Oliver and their new baby.

Like Luc and Lexi.

She'd paused outside an office—empty, I knew. Or maybe not empty any longer, I realized, seeing the new nameplate attached to the wall.

Kailey Henderson.

One piece of the puzzle solved.

Next, convincing her that she was my soul mate.

I walked up behind her, stood close as she pushed open the office door, caught the wooden panel before it shut. She didn't seem to notice that it didn't close, that I'd followed her inside.

Earbuds. Dangerous.

But I'd discuss that with her later.

I moved to the desk, leaned a hip against it, and waited

until she noticed me. Maybe she'd missed me in the hall. But in an enclosed space, this close to her person, and eventually she would spot me.

And she did.

Five minutes later.

Probably because impatience had gotten the better of me and I was rocking my leg back and forth, shaking her desk.

She stood up, pulled out her earbuds.

I opened my mouth.

"Not interested," she said.

And then she spun on her heel, pushed out through her office door, and disappeared down the hall.

TWO

Kailey

THIS WAS my own personal form of hell.

Peopling.

Twinkling lights hung overhead on the warm September evening, woven through the lush greenery of Luc and Lexi (neé Hallbright) Masterson's house.

It was the annual Breakers Team Bonding Extravaganza.

Which, I was learning, was really an excuse for a team *competition*.

Team being a group of people that apparently included me.

Not because I played hockey. Hell, I was allergic to sports. I didn't watch them, didn't play them. The closest I'd gotten to them before my friend Oliver had convinced me to uproot my life (which, admittedly, wasn't much of one, but moving to Baltimore had still been the biggest, scariest thing I'd ever done) was in P.E.

And if this was my personal hell *now*, P.E. was a special brand of hell from my past.

Soccer. Shudder. Track. Double that. Kickball. Basketball. Dodge ball—

Okay, anything with balls was bad.

Bad for me.

Bad for my glasses.

Bad for—

My gaze drifted to the right, to the big broad man who'd come into my office a week before, interest in his eyes.

Interest I'd shut down with a sharp statement.

And since then, I hadn't given him a second look.

Which was what I'd wanted. I knew men like him. I knew what men like him did with girls like me.

That being...nothing.

Maybe I looked okay on the outside.

But my inside was a mess.

A. *Mess*.

And when people got a glimpse of that mess, they ran.

Not that I could blame them.

So. Balls. Bad for me.

Moving on...to the Team Competition/Bonding Extravaganza, and the moment I'd found out that the bonding wasn't supposed to just involve the players, as I'd thought when I'd let former player (and maybe former *friend*) and my current boss, Oliver, strong-arm me into coming.

Nope.

It involved *all* the team.

Including the support staff.

Including *me*.

And if I were allergic to balls of all types, I was allergic to competition even more.

Which was why I was currently sidling toward the bushes, intending to use them as a shield before I got the hell out of there, drove home, and spent the next three hours in a bath reading my thriller and turning into a prune.

"And then"—Lexi declared, pulling out a small flower from amongst a large flat of them, a la Madame Sprout in the good ol' *HP*—"you'll pick your plant, stick it in a pot, and the person with the healthiest flower at the end of the..."

Now.

I darted, intending to slip around, escape out the open side gate—

"*Oof.*"

I bounced off something hard and big, some*one* hard and big and who smelled nice and who I was really trying to avoid because he was hot, no doubt, but he also had balls.

Unfortunately, he was also currently blocking my escape route.

"Kailey."

His voice rumbled through the air, slid down my nape, vibrated along my spine, hands coming out to steady me.

Conner Smith, defenseman for the Breakers.

My mouth opened, preparing another sharp sentiment, another barb that would keep him from getting too close.

Attack.

Run.

Safe.

My motto.

But then it happened.

It.

The most frustrating *it* in the world because I understood my triggers and tried to move past them and worked fucking hard at it to be—or at least appear like I was—a functional human being. Yeah, sometimes I wanted to sneak out of events and drown myself in my books (not the bathtub—it hadn't gotten that bad in years), but I could put on the façade of the quiet, introverted friend.

But sometimes it just happened.

A new or unforeseen trigger jumped up and latched its teeth into me, gripping me tight, shaking me roughly from side to side like a dog with a stuffed toy.

And my façade threatened to drop.

The mess threatened to escape.

Today, it was because of his thumb.

He'd steadied me, hands gripping lightly to the outsides of my arms, sitting on the sleeves of my blouse.

But his thumb...his thumb drifted down and caught my skin, the calloused fingertip making me shiver.

A strong sensation when I needed nothingness, when I needed quiet and less stimulation and for my heart that had already begun to race to chill the fuck out, for the restless energy that had been coiling inside me from the moment I'd agreed to come that night to calm. Instead, that touch of his skin to mine pulled me right into the moment, dumped me *right* back into the heaviness of what I'd been trying to escape.

The people. The noise. The obligations. The fragility of my façade.

It all tore through me.

And I couldn't snap at him. I couldn't shove him away or declare sharply that I wasn't interested in him.

I couldn't do *anything*.

"You okay?"

Couldn't speak to answer that question, couldn't step away to get away from that thumb, couldn't look away when he crouched low enough to meet my eyes, his own filled with concern.

"Kailey?" he asked again.

I barely held back my shudder.

"Come on, everyone," Lexi called. "Grab your pots and don't forget that there will be a prize for best name."

That time I couldn't hold the shudder back.

More competition. More pressure. Over a freaking name.

His brows furrowed. "Are you o—?"

"Smitty!" someone yelled, making me jump despite my spiraling efforts to hold myself together. "Come help us move this table!"

That thumb on my skin moved, and then the rest of his fingers did, tightening slightly. "Stay," he ordered. "I'll be right back."

But he didn't immediately let me go, and it took my spinning mind a moment to realize what he was waiting for.

A reply, I heard my father snap. *He's waiting for a reply, dumb shit.*

Right.

Normal people *replied*.

But I didn't have it in me for words. So instead, I just nodded.

Luckily, it was response enough for him to go away.

He released me, and my lungs loosened slightly. I turned, gaze following him as he moved toward the mass of bodies, toward the men who apparently weren't happy with the provided space for the competition and needed more space to properly plant and name their flowers.

He looked back once, eyes hitting mine, that coil in my belly tightening.

But then his lips turned up just a bit at the corners and the coil relaxed enough so that when he turned back again, grabbed one half of the table and hefted it like it weighed nothing, I took my opportunity.

I dashed out the side yard.

I made it to my car, unlocking the driver's side with shaking hands.

And then I did what I should have done the moment Oliver issued the invitation—

I ran.

Or...drove.

Escaped.

THREE

Smitty

SHE WAS GONE.

Hell, I should have known that she wouldn't stay, just because I'd asked...or okay, maybe *ask* was less than accurate. Because I'd commanded that she stay like she was a dog.

Right.

I should work on that.

But I got a little stupid when it came to one Kailey Henderson.

Probably because she had the prettiest pair of green eyes I'd ever had the privilege of seeing. Long legs and shining brown hair. Pale blue glasses that sat atop a freckle-dotted nose. A top lip fuller than the bottom. High cheekbones. Long lashes.

I'd spent a week studying her every chance I could steal a look.

And I was ready.

To convince her to give me a chance.

Yeah, I was big and clumsy and not the prettiest to look at.

But I was great at making people laugh, and I was loyal and I was strong.

I could be a good partner.

I *could.*

I just needed to prove to Kailey that despite my big and unwieldy body, my tendency to be a bit of a loose cannon on the ice, that I could be good for her.

Of course, I didn't really know her.

But I knew...nothing about her.

Shit.

That probably wasn't the best thing for a man who wanted a woman to love me.

So, plan one was to find out all the things about Kailey I could. Likes. Dislikes. All the small things that would just make her smile. All the big things that were important to her.

Then I could prove to her that I would make her happy.

I could make *someone* happy.

I *could.*

Striding out of the showers with my towel slung around my neck, I ignored the groans as I strode to my stall.

"Fuck, I didn't miss that," Raph muttered, bending over and tying his shoe.

"My glorious body?" I asked, shaking my ass, and yeah, my dick.

Which earned me more groans.

Ha.

Fuckers.

The best part of being in a locker room was being able to annoy my teammates.

Okay, the best part of this locker room was being able to play with these guys.

I could be myself.

And they might bitch and give me shit, but ever since Luc had begun making changes a few seasons ago, the team had gelled in a way that meant I'd never had a better experience, never wanted to play somewhere else.

Plus, I got to shoot a rubber disc at a net—well, at a goalie within a net—be naked a lot and in a way that didn't get me arrested, and I got to travel.

That was one of my favorite things to do.

Maybe I didn't get a ton of time to play tourist, but I had a job that brought me to different cities, and I took advantage of that.

I found the small hole-in-the-wall restaurants.

I hiked or visited random-ass museums.

I walked around, saw shit, met people.

It was epic.

The groans about my nakedness faded, and I yanked on my underwear before plunking down on the bench, reaching for my shirt and shrugging it on, closing the buttons along the front.

Then it was socks, slacks, the uncomfortable shoes.

I fucking hated suits, though I did my best to make the most of them—for example, my suit today was an epic blue and green plaid that had elicited the same groans as me coming out of the shower had.

Maybe I shouldn't like to torture my teammates...

But...meh.

It kept the locker room environment light, and up until the last couple seasons, the team had needed light.

But now we'd cut the toxic players from the roster, had won

two Cups in a row, had good management, great support staff. We were *good*.

So now we needed the room light more than ever.

Because the pressure was on and we needed a way to release it, and I didn't mind that it was me. My shoulders were big enough to carry it.

Let the guys laugh at me, groan at my antics, whine about my nakedness.

If that blew off some much-needed steam, then let that be part of my assistant captain duties.

"You coming to meet us for udon?" I asked Raph, who was shrugging into his suit jacket.

My teammate shook his head. "Nah, man. I need to get home to Monica."

Monica being the woman Raph had started dating in the off-season. She was tall, thin, blond...and had turned up pregnant.

The first three I liked about her—and really, who wouldn't? Plus, I was a fan of women in general—tall, short, curvy, slender, tits, ass, hair long or short, I liked it all. Unfortunately, it was the last, *and* the rest of her—a little snotty, a lot smirky, even more looking down her nose at me—that I didn't like as much. But my friend was happy and in fairness, I knew I was a lot. Plus, Hazel had recently been pregnant, too. I'd seen what a big change it was, and paired with the random queasiness, fatigue, and vomiting, I knew that probably made it less than fun.

Unfortunately, Monica was just...

She was a bit of a snob, okay? And she had been that way from the first time I'd met her.

So, no, I wasn't a fan.

But, though the guys thought I had a big mouth—and yeah, I did—I was also good at keeping shit inside it.

Like an opinion about the chick my teammate was dating.

Especially one who was carrying said teammate's baby.

"Yeah," I'd said, "makes sense. It's going to be hard on her when we travel, huh?"

The lines around Raph's mouth deepened. "Yeah, she's not happy about that."

See?

Here was one of the times I was able to keep shit inside my mouth.

I didn't say what I was thinking—which was: what the fuck did Monica expect, considering she was dating and had gotten knocked up by a professional hockey player?

"It can be hard on the families," was all I said.

Well, all I said before exchanging goodbyes because Raph's cell buzzed and I knew it was Monica because the man jumped and did it high, speeding through the rest of getting dressed, gathering his shit together, before hauling ass out of the locker room without a glance back.

Before, he'd sit and shoot the shit.

We'd talk about nothing and about plans for the next game, how to do better, things to try since we played on the same side of the ice.

Raph right wing.

I was right D.

Separate halves of the team, and yet it was imperative we work together.

So, we talked and planned and rehashed and thought ahead to who we were playing against, and since I liked to talk—about anything really—but also especially about hockey, I missed having that with Raph.

But he had a girl at home, a kid on the way.

Things were going to change.

So I had better get used to it.

Nothing stayed the same.

Before I could ruminate on that, wonder why that was bothering me so much, Theo, one of the younger guys on the team and currently getting his degree in Zoology, said something about the mating habits of camels that required me to *not* keep my mouth shut.

And then there were more groans and sock balls being thrown and shit being given and a group of us getting ready to go out to get udon.

And I stopped thinking about the disquiet that had been sitting heavily on my chest ever since—

A sock ball beaned me right in the face, and I couldn't even be mad.

I was relieved to not think about that source of disquiet.

Still, I snagged it and yeeted it back at my current D partner, Cas. He was a good friend, a pain in the ass, and there was no way in hell that I was going to let the indignity of a sock ball to the face stand.

No fucking way.

I grabbed it, rolled it tighter, and...let it rip.

FOUR

Kailey

NORMALLY, I would be in my own world, not noticing the noise that came from the locker room.

Making a special effort to avoid the locker room altogether.

To not even be on the same side of the building.

Because there were naked men in there.

Because...there was a naked *Conner Smith* in there.

And as I was now part of the team, I had all sorts of inside information about the team. Including knowing that Smitty enjoyed being naked.

That...

Created all sorts of problems—at least inside my head. Because I'd thought of the deep brown eyes, the mouth quirking beneath his thick beard, his strong hands steadying me...

Way too much in the last few days.

He'd gotten into my head.

And *that* spelled trouble.

I could blame it on a weird spell or the aforementioned *trouble* or just Conner being Conner. Or, I supposed, I could blame it on the fact that after my meeting with Luc and Oliver and several people from the social media strategy team about the new app the Breakers wanted to release to the public, I'd been off my game due to too much peopling. Or I could place that blame on Luc asking me to stay after that meeting, remaining in his office and talking about some bugs that had come up in the program I'd built to track player development, the reason I was here in Baltimore in the first place, drawing on my already faltering reserves and making my head a little muzzy.

Because now, it was late, and I was tired.

But I was going back to my office to get my purse, and instead of going home, I was going to Hazel and Oliver's place.

Food.

A boardgame.

Cuddling with baby Dominic, who wouldn't judge me for being weird.

Checking out Oliver's new gaming computer. He'd just finished building it and considering we'd first met in an online Discord chat about one of our favorite games and had become virtual friends *way* before real-life friends, eating food, playing a game, and checking out some tech sounded like my idea of perfection...

Only second to spending the night alone in my bath with my book.

I was thinking about his processor, wondering if it'd be able to handle the latest update of the game we both still played, happy to be in my head for a little while because it meant that I could escape a bit from the socializing of the meeting.

Oliver was okay.

Luc...was problematic. Not that I didn't like him. I did. A

lot, actually. He was really cool and easy going and super smart. But he was my boss, in a way that was clearly my boss, not in the sort-of-friend, sort-of-boss way that described my working relationship with Oliver.

He let me do my thing.

I did my thing.

There wasn't a lot of boss-employee overlap with our friendship.

With Luc, there was no overlap.

He was my *boss*. Well, actually, he was my boss's *boss* and so that put him firmly in the category of scary and anxiety-inducing. Would I say something that would be weird or awkward or put Oliver's job at risk? He'd vouched for me, and I *could* be weird, so...

And that wasn't even including all the weird things I could say that would hurt my own chances in this new position.

Or might *not* say.

Like what if I was spinning so rapidly in my own head that I didn't respond in time and then I'd look like an idiot and—

Meetings were exhausting.

All that being said, I wasn't really paying attention to where I was going when I realized I was walking by the locker room.

The locker room with the naked men...and based on the rumbling voice echoing out into the hall, the naked Conner Smith.

"Fuck," I whispered, feet slowing, teeth coming to my bottom lip.

I pressed hard, the bite of pain clearing the fog in my brain.

Of course, I couldn't just stand there in the hall, biting my lip and wringing my hands. I needed to get the fuck out of there and I needed to do it fast and—

Deep breath.

Just walk by.

I wasn't creeping.

I belonged here and I wouldn't look and—

Right.

Shit. Someone was coming around the corner at the far end of the hall and if I *did* continue to stand here staring off into space, I *would* look like a creeper and then I'd be fired, and then I would probably get Oliver fired and—

Fuck, Kailey. Move your ass.

Right. Okay. I could do that.

Lean forward, use gravity to my advantage, start my feet moving, and *go*. Eyes forward. Gaze not drifting toward the open locker room door (*no fucking way, Henderson!*). Go. Go. *Go!*

I went.

Wall. Wall. Opening. Not looking. Not looking. Not lo—

"Oof!"

Every bit of the air in my lungs left in a rush as I found myself colliding with something hard...and big...and broad... and a handsome, bearded face with deep brown eyes and black hair, with plump lips and a scar across his temple.

I collided with Smitty.

And, fuck, he smelled good.

Spicy and manly, his body close to mine, his expression going from shock to horror in the blink of an eye. And literally, in the blink of an eye was how long it took for me to process that I *hadn't* avoided him, that I was standing smack dab in the open doorway.

Or had been, anyway.

Because now I was *falling* right in front of that open door-way, Conner's broad body taking me out as efficiently as he'd laid out players on opposing teams.

His broad hands held something blue and white, but that

was all I could see before his fingers opened, whatever he held dropped to the floor. Before he reached for me. Before time seemed to speed up again.

Only, he was too late.

He made a valiant effort, hands reaching for me.

But I was falling and in another blink of that eye, I hit the industrial carpeting hard.

Maybe if I'd fallen to the black skate mat on the public side of the locker room (where they let media in and the occasional fan or visitor) it wouldn't have hurt so much. But this was the private side of the space. Where the guys changed and showered. They didn't need thick rubber mats to protect their edges because they wore shoes here, not skates.

This was concrete with a thin layer of durable carpet.

This meant that getting checked to it by a player who outweighed me by a good hundred pounds and was taller than me by an entire foot hurt like hell.

The air had been knocked out of my lungs by the initial impact but dropping to the floor somehow shook free a few more air molecules. Then I wasn't thinking about air or my lungs or even the floor. I was just gritting my teeth together and blinking back tears.

"Fuck," Smitty whispered, dropping to his knees at my side, his hands outstretched.

He didn't touch me, just sort of floated them through the air, as though he were going to magically heal me through his palms. Either that, or he was scared to touch me again. "Kailey, sweetheart, are you okay?" Then he did touch me, his palm resting lightly on my arm. "I'm so sorry. I didn't see you walking by."

That wasn't a surprise.

People didn't normally see me.

People who weren't this man anyway.

"Kay?" Concern on his face, in the V of his brows. "Are you okay?" A beat. "Do I need to get Samantha?"

Samantha?

Wait. That was the trainer. The woman who would presumably be able to confirm if I was concussed because a six-foot-six-inch, two-hundred-twenty-pound (yes, I'd looked up his stats) hockey player had taken me out.

I *felt* concussed.

I *felt* broken.

Getting knocked down by that big hockey player wasn't a sport, or at least not one I wanted to be part of, especially since it *fucking* hurt.

But getting checked out for concussions would mean drawing this out.

Would mean more peopling.

So, no, that couldn't happen.

I put my hands beneath me and shoved up, ignoring the throbbing pain in my hip. Warm palms gripped my arms before I made it to my feet, helping me the rest of the way.

Smitty's concerned face dropped into view. "Kailey, honey, talk to me."

And, fuck, wouldn't that be *easy?*

To just be able to open my mouth and say the right thing would be fucking *incredible.*

But that wasn't *me.*

I sucked in a breath, closed my eyes. It was easier that way. It was *better.* "Please, let go."

The words were barely audible, especially with the noise in the locker room, teasing and yelling and the odd, "What, Smitty? It's not bad enough that you lay people out on the ice, now you have to do it off as well?"

But he heard me.

Because his big body went still, and his hands opened.

And I was free.

"Do you need a doctor?" he asked quietly.

My eyes remained closed, and I slowly shook my head. "No." It was raspy. Garbled. But a sound that was a word. And that helped me take a breath in, to let it out. Free my lungs, my throat, my tongue. "No," I said again. "I'm fine."

A pause.

But though my lids were firmly shut, I knew he hadn't gone. Not when I could *feel* him.

On my skin, his now-quiet presence prickling along my nerve endings.

In my stomach, swirling and tightening.

"Will you look at me?" he asked softly.

Fuck.

"No," I whispered

More quiet.

Then a breath.

Then, "I'm going to back away," he said, "and I know you want me to leave you alone, and I will, but I'm going to make sure you can move okay first and aren't going to pass out."

My tongue pressed hard to the roof of my mouth.

"All right?"

No.

Not *all right*.

But also, my tongue wasn't working and that was all I had and—

Right.

I needed to get out of this.

So...I nodded.

My eyes stayed closed as I felt his presence lessen, the heat that surrounded him, that was disconcerting me so intensely, cooled slightly as he backed away.

But my feet didn't move, and my eyes didn't open and—

"Go on, Kay."

Right.

I dropped my chin to my chest, forced my eyes to open, blinking against the bright lights of the hall until the pale gray of my shoelaces came into focus.

Then I tilted my head up—avoiding the big man altogether, though I did get a glimpse of a wide expanse of ugly plaid— before turning and moving down the hall.

It hurt, but I did my best to pretend it didn't, to move normally and smoothly.

I had the feeling he knew it hurt anyway.

FIVE

Smitty

I SHOVED my keys into my pocket, shrugged into my jacket.

Took a breath, the atmosphere of the locker room continuing on without me, and then I left. They'd probably wonder why I bailed on food when I—as a six-foot-plus, two-hundred-twenty-pound behemoth *never* bailed on food.

But, hell, I already spent a lot of time feeling like an asshole.

A big, goofy, giant asshole.

Today, I'd earned those inner thoughts.

Knocking Kailey to the ground, and she despised me so much that I couldn't even help her up, steady her, *touch* her. And right, she didn't owe me anything, didn't have to allow me to do anything for her.

But...I *wanted* her to.

I'd felt the pieces inside me shift when I'd first seen her, as though all the cells in my body had realigned, focused completely on her, and in my typical way, I'd assumed that I'd just need to spend some time with her, that I'd be able to win her over, and then we'd have the happily ever after that Luc and Oliver and Marcel had.

Meet woman.

Woman falls for me.

Happy ending.

Done.

Easy.

Except, I thought as I moved into the hallway, this time being careful to watch out for tiny green-eyed, brown-haired beauties, *not* easy.

"Yo, Smitty!"

I glanced up from the carpet—yeah, I'd been staring at it like Kailey might reappear and give me a second chance to help her up—and saw Oliver coming down the hall.

"I'm not taking care of your plant," I said, fist-bumping Oliver's outstretched hand. "I don't care how busy you are now that you're married with a kid on the way."

"I'd never ask that," Oliver replied dryly. "I went to the plant funeral last season, remember?"

Ah. Yes. Our annual tradition to play dirges and take the long, solemn walk to the compost bin, followed by the long, solemn walk back, avoiding Lexi's disapproving gaze.

"Hey! It's not my fault that there was a freak snowstorm and—"

"You left an indoor plant outside so poor little Sally froze to death?"

Yes, I'd named my plant Sally. Yes, I'd murdered poor little Sally by leaving her out in the elements for two days—*cough*—weeks. But how was I supposed to know that she couldn't survive a little cold and snow? For fuck's sake, she was supposed to be a Maryland native and—

"Or that Hazel told me your petunia this season was already looking droopy?"

Fuck.

How did she know?

Oh...right, she'd come over to my house with some papers she wanted me to fill out the night before. Personality test nonsense and some things for me to read.

Homework to get me mentally prepared for the season.

Yay.

I *loved* homework.

And yes, that was me being not-so-subtle, as usual.

School and my brain didn't fit. I wasn't dumb, not by any means, but I was dyslexic and that made it challenging to read for fun...or for homework-slash-work-work personality tests that were important because they were critical to the flow of the team and because Hazel was the shit and had asked me to complete them because they were important to her.

Still, no joke, Marcel had gotten to go to a wreck room and bust shit up.

I'd gotten homework.

Probably, if I'd disclosed the fact that sometimes the letters swam on the page and or flipped themselves over or decided to look like another letter, she wouldn't have given me the packets.

But I hadn't told anyone that.

Hadn't let it define my life in a long time.

Not since I'd thought that dyslexia had *made* me dumb. Not since everyone around me had thought the same.

Big. Oafish. Dumb.

Those three went together.

"My guess is that you either over or under-watered her," Oliver was saying. "Are the edges of her leaves changing colors?"

I narrowed my eyes, stopped thinking about my fucked-up brain. "Why do I feel like you're sabotaging me already?"

A wolfish smile. "Because I'm going to win this competition again?"

"Theo won last year," I pointed out.

That smile faded. "Only because I wasn't competing."

I leaned back against the wall, crossed my arms. "Why do I feel like you have a big part to do with the entire organization now growing flowers?"

"I have no idea what you're talking about," Oliver said innocently.

Right.

He just wanted to regain possession of Mac, an adorably ugly (and very creepy) underwear-wearing, plastic teeth-sporting blue creature that he'd won in the first plant contest and had to give up to Theo since the studious forward had won last season.

I didn't give a shit about Mac—though, if I did somehow manage to not kill the flower with my black thumb, I would be damn sure to take my bragging rights to the nth degree.

Everyone would be hearing about my victory.

But since that wouldn't happen, I'd just do my best to draw out the planticide for as long as possible.

Poor little petunia was fucked.

"Well," I said, "as illuminating as this conversation is, I *do* need to go."

Oliver stopped, brows drawing together. "Aren't you going to dinner with the guys?"

Right. Fuck. I probably assumed that considering that was what I always did, but I'd snuck out and I was going home to lick my wounds and...

"I'm actually a little tired."

Hell.

Now concern registered on Oliver's face.

Fuck. I should have known better. I was *never* tired. I prided myself on being an Energizer Bunny who never stopped, on the ice and in the locker room and at home and—

It would warrant concern I didn't want to draw if I was tired.

Fuck.

"I'm a little out of shape"—lie, I'd been working my ass off—"so I want to get to bed early." That didn't erase the concern. "Plus, your wife gave me *homework* last night."

That set a dumb look on Oliver's face.

Which I took full advantage of.

"I don't want to disappoint Hazel"—that part was true—"and I'm supposed to meet her tomorrow, so I want to get it done."

Thankfully, that worked.

The dumb expression spread into dazed and determined and *lovestruck*.

A pang in my gut.

Yearning to look like that kind of idiot.

"So, I'm gonna go, yeah?"

Oliver nodded, still a little distracted by thoughts of his woman, so I took advantage of that distraction, clapped my buddy on the shoulder, said my goodbyes, then got the fuck out of there before someone else could stop me.

Out of the practice facility.

Into my car.

Down the highway.

To my house.

And then I did what I always did when I felt like this.

I dropped my shit on the counter, grabbed a flashlight and a granola bar, and I walked straight out my back door.

SIX

Kailey

I SMILED AT OLIVER, pressed my finger to my lips, and tilted my head toward the door.

Hazel, Dominic cradled on her chest, both of them sound asleep.

Oliver's wife had dozed off sometime during me and Oliver droning on about memory and graphics cards, Dominic dozing off right alongside her, his little fist pressed to his mouth.

I knew from personal experience earlier in the evening that the fist in Dominic's mouth paired with him falling asleep would mean that a puddle of drool would be left behind when he woke up.

Lucky for little Mr. Dominic, he was really freaking cute, so I hadn't minded the stain left behind.

But now, two out of the three members of the house were sleeping, and I'd already eaten and admired Oliver's computer. It was time for me to go.

Leave the happy family to it.

Oliver caught my arm. "You don't have to."

I patted his hand. "Get your wife and son to bed," I murmured. "I'm going to go home and play *Legends of the Dragons* until I can't keep my eyes open."

A sigh. "Lucky." He made a face. "I hardly have time to play anymore."

"No," I said lightly. "You're the lucky one."

His expression gentled. "Yeah, Kay, I am."

He knew it. He never let Hazel doubt that truth, and I knew that he would never allow Dominic to doubt that same truth. Oliver loved him, would always love him, even despite the flaws that every person had, despite making mistakes as he no doubt would, despite not being perfect or not sleeping through the night and leaving drool stains on T-shirts.

And I didn't have that.

So, I wouldn't let Oliver waste it.

A squeeze of his hand before gently peeling back his fingers. "Bed, Ollie," I murmured. "And give them a hug and kiss from me."

He nodded, stepped back.

Then stopped. "Kailey?"

"Yeah?" I murmured.

"I know that the social stuff is hard for you..."

Immediately, my stomach began knotting, clenching and rolling, and winding tighter and tighter.

"...but"—he moved over to me, the motion so smooth no one would have ever known he'd lost his leg after a horrific on-ice hit not long ago—"you're really cool, yeah? The team, any one of us you want to let in, would be lucky to know you."

My lungs expanded.

"No pressure," he said softly. "Just if or when you feel ready, yeah?"

Lungs tight again. My tongue glued to the roof of my mouth.

But I managed to nod.

Then I turned for the door, slipped through, and walked into the cool night air.

I TURNED on the taps of the bath, dipping my fingers into the stream of water, waving them around to ensure the temperature was right before plugging the tub.

It was late.

I'd spent too long with the new update, flying around in my virtual dragon form, pillaging enemy villages, and saving the villagers under my protection. By the time I'd finished with my quest, it was after midnight, and I'd increased my gold hoard to the point that I'd needed to upgrade my den.

Plush carpets, an oversized fireplace (because dragons liked it hot), and plenty of storage for my shiny trinkets.

My virtual world was expansive, and I wished that I could speak as well with my mouth in real life as I did with my fingers in that online life. They moved fast and of their own accord, not needing the awkward pauses, the over-analyzing. Just type out a response and go.

If only my freaking mouth would work as well in real life.

In fact, the only person that I *had* that with—and it was still a bastardized copy of my online self—was with Oliver.

We'd talked online so much over the years and about work so much recently, that a lot of the awkwardness had dissipated. I was still...Kailey. Still paused too often, avoided eye contact, felt uncomfortable in my own skin.

But I *could* talk.

It was a little weird at times (but that was me). It took me a bit to relax (*also* me).

But it was as normal as I got.

Books. Coding. Playing my game. Those were all easy. Soaking in a bath until I turned into a prune. Even more so.

A big, bearded man with a penchant for loud plaid, an infectious smile, and a sudden interest in me?

Uh...yeah, that was definitely *not* natural.

It was also...unwanted.

Right?

I was happy in my bubble, settling in, expanding a little bit with events like the team get-together. My parents were on the other side of the country and though the move had seemed overwhelming at first, I could say now that it was the right thing to have done.

A full-time gig with my closest real-life-online friend.

People who were cool and smart and talented and who pushed me a little but backed off when I needed them to.

Opportunities to be involved.

Plenty of space to soothe the part of me that needed it.

So yeah, I still had moments where the anxiety gripped me tight and made it hard to do the simplest things, like just remain on the fringes of a party, watching the others interact, to engage in small talk or friendly competitions.

But...away from my dad, I was better.

My cell rang.

Right.

I'd thought of him and conjured up the monster with just that internal musing.

Ring.

"Shit," I whispered, eyeing my bath, the steam rising off the water in curling tendrils, debating and knowing that it was better to bite the bullet and just answer the call.

Get it over with.

Be done for this segment of time so I wouldn't have to talk to him again.

Sighing, I dried my hands on the towel, picked up my cell, and swiped.

Lifted it to my ear.

"What took you so long?" blasted through the speaker before I even had a chance to open my mouth and say hello.

"Hi, Da—"

"I was sitting there listening to the phone ring," he snapped. "I'm very busy and I'm taking time out of my day to call my daughter—who, by the way, *never* calls me—and I'm just standing here with my dinner getting cold, twiddling my goddamned thumbs, and listening to the phone ringing, and— Jesus Christ, Kailey, *just say something*."

Just say *something*.

A familiar sentiment.

But, God, so fucking hard when he was always like that.

Impatient. Snapping. Expecting.

My kryptonite.

"I'm here, Dad," I managed to croak out.

"I know *that*," he said. "I called. You picked up. Now my dinner is getting cold. Tell me about work and what you've been doing with your time."

Okay, I'd forgotten about commanding.

A command to speak was just as bad as the impatience and snapping and expectant tone. The four coming together to form a quad-fecta (was that a word? I didn't think so, but it fit well enough, anyway) of anxiety-inducing gloriousness.

Then again that was my father.

"Kailey." A whip of my name. "*Speak*."

Like I was a dog, and if only that command would work, just to get the freaking man off my back.

Already I was sweating, moisture gathering in my armpits, between my breasts, trickling down my spine. My tongue was thick and dry. My throat swollen and closing more and more by the moment.

A sigh, nearly as whiplike as my name had been.

"I see this new job hasn't improved your communication skills at all." Another sigh and I could picture him with one palm flat on his kitchen island, fork in the other, cell pinned between shoulder and ear, his plate of chicken and steamed broccoli growing cold in front of him. Always the same food. Always so structured. Always growing cold as he yelled at me.

And then he wouldn't even reheat it.

Because then the chicken breast would get tough and the broccoli mushy.

Not that he would stop calling me at this time.

It would deprive him of the opportunity to belittle me.

Which, *look,* I understood—not the belittling, because that was shitty and I might have anxiety and be shy and have trouble with socializing, but I was a human being and deserved respect. Being quiet, having difficulty speaking up didn't mean I was stupid or weak, like he often insinuated. The part I did understand was that belittling was his tactic and he wouldn't stop doing it.

It made him feel big or important or smarter than me.

Or maybe it was just so much a part of his personality that he wouldn't ever stop it.

Or both.

Probably both.

"Are you even practicing the techniques I paid all that money for you to have from that overpriced therapist?"

He'd paid for five therapy appointments.

When I was thirteen.

He'd refused to come in for a parent meeting, had just told my therapist—in front of me—to "fix her" and then he'd left.

Five hours was not enough time to unpack what my father was.

It certainly wasn't enough time to help me manage my anxiety.

But my therapist had tried, then had set me up with the counselor at school.

And I knew those five hours and the weekly twenty minutes with the busy school counselor had been the reason I'd gotten through high school.

Survived by the skin of my teeth.

Then a scholarship to Stanford, finding my groove with engineering and math, not being the smartest, but being surrounded by weird, smart people like me.

Online friends.

Classes that challenged my mind.

Helping me understand that I deserved the respect I hadn't realized up until that point was so lacking.

Pulling back from my family.

Going to therapy again, this time paid for by my tech industry job. Picking up side projects for apps and websites that made my heart sing.

Understanding the abuse.

Pulling back further.

But it was nearly impossible to cut ties with someone who owned a private jet. If I didn't talk to him once a week, he'd fly out, show up on my porch, and berate me in person.

The calls were easier.

Plus, it made everything in my life seem easier after dealing with the maelstrom that was my father.

"I'm using my techniques," I said calmly. "And I'm glad that you're doing well—"

"You haven't even asked how I'm doing."

My molars grinding together. My spine straightening. My free hand clenching. But calm, and words were working now, so I was going to keep going with that. "How are you doing, Dad?"

"Terrible," he grumbled. "I'm too busy and now the company wants to offer me a promotion. I asked them how they expected that I take on more responsibility and *they* responded by opening their checkbooks."

"That's...great." It sounded like hell for the employees who worked under him, but my father had been with the company for almost twenty years, so what did I know?

Maybe they liked pompous assholes.

And considering they'd kept him around for two decades, I supposed that was true.

He prattled on, telling me about the money (extensive), his new department he was taking over ("a complete mess filled with idiots"), and his golf game (the only meaningful hobby in his opinion).

The prattling and complaining—all loud, all intense, all making my teeth clench together, my spine prickle—cut off precisely ten minutes later.

Ten *eternal* minutes later.

But my dad had a time limit.

Ten minutes to check in with his children per week.

So, I endured. Managed to get in a few more responses, which I knew my father barely heard, but which were important for me because I needed practice engaging in uncomfortable conversations.

One day, I wanted to be in a situation that would normally trigger me and be able to handle it with aplomb.

That was my dream.

And maybe it was a small one.

But when my father brushed me off the phone as quickly as he'd engaged me—those ten minutes up—and I put my cell down, I knew that I was going to do it someday.

Keep working.

Keep getting better.

Keep trying.

Keep avoiding the type of men who were big and loud and would stifle me, who would prevent all my hard work from meaning anything.

Keep avoiding Conner Smith.

Because he would crush me.

SEVEN

I GRUNTED as I hooked the bar onto the supports, sweat dripping down my temples, my chest, my back.

Fucking hard work staying in shape.

I just wanted to eat pizza and sushi, lift the TV remote and a beer instead of dumbbells and doing bench presses. I wanted my cardio to be fucking.

There was nothing like having a woman in my lap, her naked body pressed to mine.

Hips and ass and breasts and curves.

Floral-scented shampoo and shining brown hair, bright green eyes.

Okay, I wanted Kailey in my lap, Kailey naked in my bed. But...she didn't like me. I needed to realize that, get over it.

Sure.

Tell that to my dick that had woken me up at four in the morning, rock hard and weeping after I'd spent most of the night dreaming about Kailey and what she'd look like naked and in my bed...naked and *coming* in my bed.

There was a reason I was in the weight room, lifting until my arms shook, running on the treadmill until my legs felt like rubber, and the sun wasn't even up yet.

Practice that day was going to be hell.

But...I had to do something.

And if exercising until my dick got soft was the only something I could think of, then so be it. My body would appreciate it as the season went on.

Stay strong.

Stay healthy.

Stay—

My cock twitched.

Hard, apparently.

Sigh.

Wiping my face with a towel, I stood, moved out of my weight room (which was really just my office with my desk shoved into one corner that I'd stopped using as an office because I always ended up doing any work on my couch, my laptop—and sadly, *not* a woman—plunked on my lap). Up the stairs to my bedroom and into the shower, giving in approximately thirty seconds after stepping into the scalding stream, wrapping my fingers around my cock, gripping tight, stroking fast and hard, coming in an embarrassingly short amount of time considering I'd done just this same thing after getting back from my hike the night before.

Four hours and I could barely hold out for a minute?

I was in trouble.

Especially since I was fantasizing about a certain green-eyed brunette who wanted nothing to do with me.

I'd barely come, but just those green eyes appearing in my mind was enough for my cock to get hard again.

Cute.

As in, I was either going to walk around with permanent blue balls, or I was going to get tendinitis from whacking it so much to relieve it.

Ignoring my dick—because short of getting to work on that tendinitis, that was all I had. *Embrace the blue balls, Smitty! That's all you're going to get!*

Why did my inner asshole always sound like the announcers at the rink?

No clue.

Except that hockey had been my life for so long that I pretty much always thought in references.

Except that hockey had been the only reason I'd made it through school, my only motivation when the letters flowed around the page, that they flipped upside down or twisted onto themselves or rotated over backward. It didn't matter that it always took me a long time to finish reading a book, even though I was enjoying the story.

I could just get out on the ice and skate my ass off.

And that would be enough.

Work hard. Hit hard. Get the fucking puck and get it up to my teammates so they can score.

Shoot from the blue line. Hope someone would tip it in.

Protect my goalie, my teammates.

Fight and check. Stay on my skates. Clear the crease.

None of those required doing something I wasn't good at.

But what I had to do next did.

Hazel's homework. I'd tried to summon the energy to look at the packet the night before. Really, I had.

But I'd been feeling so fucking down, like such a goddamned loser.

Kailey didn't like me.

I liked her.

Why? Why did it matter? Why did I care? Why did I think I had a right to her affection?

Newsflash, I fucking didn't.

But people *liked* me, and—

"Fuck, man," I muttered, yanking my hands through my hair, twisting the handle for the shower hard enough that it groaned in protest when I turned off the water.

Rough hands using my towel to dry off the pertinent bits, ignoring my dick.

Throwing on clothes and was thankful I could wear sweats and a T-shirt to the rink that day instead of a fucking suit. Socks and shoes on. Hoodie over my head.

Down the stairs.

To my laptop, still sitting on the coffee table where I'd dumped it last night, frustrated that I was so off my game that my normal strategies for reading and working weren't useful.

Opening the top, dropping onto the couch.

The screen brightened, illuminating the document, and... fuck it, I couldn't sit down and deal with that again.

I needed to get out of the house.

Needed to clear my head and not do this here.

Grabbing my laptop, I shoved it into my backpack, threw it over my shoulder, and got the hell out of my house.

THIRTY MINUTES LATER, I was at the practice rink—well, at the player's snack area that was tucked away between the locker rooms and the training suites and various offices.

It was really just a conference room filled with recliners and couches, a small kitchen shoved against the back wall. Food was either made by the staff at certain times, or—like now—there was stuff we could fix ourselves. A Keurig for coffee, pastries from a local bakery, a fridge stocked with fruits and veggies and lean protein. Packets of oatmeal and various cereals.

For the guys who were used to all forms of continental breakfasts, it was a familiar spread of items.

For me, who'd been up since four and yet to have coffee, it was a welcome—and empty—sight.

"Fuck," I muttered, shoving a pod into the coffee maker and grabbing a mug so I could brew myself a much-needed cup. I needed to take advantage of the empty and get my broodiness out, get back to myself, stop caring that Kailey didn't like me, accept that she wasn't *going* to like me, so the guys didn't know that I was all twisted up inside.

Because despite all the talk, I couldn't do acceptance about Kailey.

I just...didn't have it in me.

But, okay, here was the deal. I knew I was going to accept that she wasn't going to like me *romantically*. I wasn't that much of an asshole to expect a woman to fall for me just because I was bordering on obsessed.

In a perfect world? Yes.

In a world where I was him—a big brute who was only good at hitting things with my fists or stick or puck and, okay, I was also good at finding hole-in-the-wall restaurants—but I was fully aware that I wasn't a catch like pretty Marcel or supremely talented like Raph and Oliver were. I did okay. I ground it out, got shit done, knew I had an important role in the locker room.

But I wasn't going to be gracing billboards or be in the All-Star game.

I hit shit and made people laugh, and I did both of those things well.

So, her not falling madly in love with me, that I could deal with.

But I *wasn't* going to stop until she liked me as a friend.

I was a good friend. I could be that for her, and even if it wasn't all I wanted it to be, it would be enough for me.

"Good plan, Smitty," I muttered, scooping the cup off the Keurig and feeling a million times better as I snooped in the pastry box, loaded up on apple turnovers, and then went to one of the recliners. Since I was in the room first, I had full control of the remote, and I clicked on the TV, immediately shuddering when I saw it was paused on some weird-ass documentary about Australian animals, a wombat waddling across the screen.

The marsupials creeped me the fuck out, and I knew it was either Theo studying up on something, or one of the guys trying to mess with me.

Either way, I was messed with.

Whoever thought they were cute little critters had clearly lost their minds.

First, they had a pouch.

Second, they had scary-ass claws.

Third, they had beady black eyes.

Fourth...none of this was getting me any closer to completing my personality test.

"Fuck."

A sigh.

A glug of coffee.

"Okay, dumbass"—a breath—"just get this done."

EIGHT

Kailey

I WAS WALKING down the hall, heading for my office, when I heard it.

Muttering.

Angry muttering.

Considering I was party to my own muttering—and it wasn't a little amount, especially when I was trying to troubleshoot a project—I'd been prepared to walk by.

Silently.

Without making eye contact and disappearing directly into my office, closing the door, and breathing easy because I hadn't had to people.

But as I got closer, I recognized the rumbling.

Or rather, *who* was rumbling.

And my pulse began tap-dancing in my veins.

Don't look. Don't look. Don't—

I looked.

Right into the lounge area, the kitchen deserted behind

Smitty, the lights on, but dimly because he was the only one in the space.

And he was muttering and cursing and tearing his hands through his hair.

God, he was big.

I shouldn't have forgotten that, not with how he'd knocked me down the day before (hell, my hip was still sore and reminding me that I wouldn't be able to hold my own against him on the ice, or off it). I shouldn't have forgotten how big he was, not with how he towered over me at the party or in the hall.

But what really drove his size home—

And yes, my eyes went to a certain location, and that location was something that I assumed was equally as large as the rest of him.

Not that I could see it.

Oh, what a girl wouldn't give for X-ray vision.

Was that too much to ask for?

Just one little peek to satisfy my curiosity and then *moving on.*

He shifted and I jumped, realized I was staring at his crotch, and jerked my gaze back up to what had caught my focus after the muttering and before the dick considering— Smitty was *big.* Thankfully, he was too distracted by the computer in his lap to have noticed me stopping and doing all that dick considering, too distracted now to see me staring over at him.

But...I'd sat in those chairs.

They weren't the normal family room variety.

They were made for big guys.

And he practically overflowed the pale brown leather armchair.

How?

Which *so* didn't matter, I knew. Definitely didn't have any bearing on my current life. Shouldn't even be in my thoughts, considering I was trying to erect plenty of distance between us.

Shaking my head, I started to move on.

Would have moved on.

If I hadn't heard...

"Come on, you fucking idiot, this shouldn't be this hard."

Quiet. Hissed words.

Directed at himself.

But they might as well have been directed at me. God knew, I'd heard similar ones often enough, had felt the barbed words slice through me.

Had probably worn the same expression he now wore more times than I could count.

Because what was on his face was what I'd felt in my gut so often.

So *fucking* often that I stopped.

So *fucking* often that I stepped into that empty—save one Conner Smith—room and sucked in a breath.

"Just fucking do it," he gritted.

My heart began to pound, clunking against my rib cage, palms going sweaty, knees practically knocking together.

But...somehow the words came.

"Can I help you?"

"Just fucking—" The sentence skidded to a halt, his mouth dropping open, eyes flying up to mine. "Kailey?" he whispered.

Oh boy, what was I doing?

It was a lot harder to actually look into his deep brown eyes, to be in front of him offering help, knowing that was counterintuitive to everything I'd been preaching to myself in my head since he'd first approached me.

But...I couldn't just walk by.

Couldn't leave him with frustration etched on his face, mixing with sad, with fury, with...old pain.

"I—"

My throat closed up. That ball of anxiety began expanding in my gut, clawing its way up my torso, digging its talons into my lungs, my neck, my tongue.

It took everything in me to remain in place and just breathe.

And as everything else inside of me spun like a tornado, I was just standing there. Staring at him.

If I'd seen one glimpse of impatience, I would have shut down, would have lost it and run. But there wasn't any impatience. Just deep brown eyes on mine, searching my gaze for answers, *waiting* for me to speak.

My heart skipped a beat, but this time it wasn't anxiety-induced.

It was...

Smitty.

Chocolate eyes. Thick beard. A scar through his right eyebrow. Gentle *all* over his face.

I tried again. "I..."

And still he waited.

And...somehow, that made it okay. "I'm sorry to intrude," I said softly. "I just...did you need any help—" Something warm entered his eyes, and I found myself unable to hold them, my gaze dropping to his lap (and not to the shadows concealing what I hoped was a monster dick this time).

Monster dick?

Christ, I was losing my mind.

Swallowing hard, I managed to press on. "I just"—another breath—"I'm good with computers and can help if..."

That was the end of my words. I just ran out of steam. Eyes flicking up, I braced.

But Smitty didn't snap at me.

Instead, he studied my like I was a puzzle he didn't get. For a long time, his gaze stayed on my face.

Then he said, "No. You can't help me."

It was like he'd taken a pin and popped a balloon inside me, all the air just streaming out of me, deflating me in a slow, steady outflow.

"Right," I whispered then started to turn. "I'll just go—"

"I'm dyslexic."

My feet slid to a stop, I turned back. "What?" I whispered.

"I'm a dyslexic," he murmured.

"I'm..." A breath, that knot in my stomach slowly loosening. "I'm not sure what that means," I whispered, shifting slowly from foot to foot. "I mean, I've heard of being dyslexic and I had a friend in high school who told me that the letters moved on the page sometimes. Is that—?" I glanced up, held his eyes. "Is that what's making it hard this morning?"

A nod to his computer.

Tension in the air, balling in his shoulders, in the heavy weight of his frame. "Yes," he said. "Reading isn't the easiest for me in general."

"Why?"

My teeth hit my bottom lip.

That was a shitty question.

It wasn't any of my business. It would be like someone asking me why I got anxious sometimes. Who the fuck knew? My body was just my body, and my brain worked the way it worked and...sigh...it was kind of douchey to just expect that there was an easier explanation.

Smitty shifted, closing his laptop and setting it in the chair next to him. "I have surface dyslexia," he said. "So, it's a lot like what your friend described—the letters shifting and moving and twisting in on themselves. And then what I see for a letter sometimes isn't the same as what everyone else sees."

"What do you mean?"

He tapped at a sticker on the back of his laptop, a large black and blue rendering of the Breakers logo. "You probably see all of the letters as whole, yeah?"

I nodded.

A finger to the B. "This sometimes looks like a three to me. I know there's supposed to be a line here. Sometimes I see it, but sometimes I don't. And then sometimes those letters, even when they *are* whole, move and twist in on themselves like I'm high."

He sighed.

"That's what's been happening this morning." A beat. "And last night."

"But sometimes it doesn't?"

Smitty was quiet. "I've done a lot of work to get to a point where I can read effectively"—a self-deprecating smile—"and some days it's easier than others."

"What makes it easier?" I asked, knowing I was pushing boundaries, but genuinely curious about this man who was so big and loud and yet sitting alone in a room at seven in the morning, yelling at himself about reading something on his laptop, twin tracks in his hair, mussed from frustrated swipes.

He patted the chair next to him.

And...I sat.

And listened.

"Usually, shorter bursts of reading are better," he said softly. "And the font and background color both matter." A sigh. "And not getting irritated or frustrated at myself."

I giggled. "I'm not so sure that has been working." A nod to his hair. "Considering you've been trying to pull your hair out."

Silence.

Brown eyes on mine.

A curl in my gut slowly tightening.

Fuck. I'd overstepped again.

Then he smiled, chuckled in a low, rasping way that had goose bumps prickling on my nape, heat replacing the tightness in my stomach. "Yeah, Kay. You've got that right, and add in the fact that I haven't been sleeping well and that I need to finish this before my meeting with Hazel, and...it's a disaster for my luscious locks."

Self-deprecating again.

Paired with a disarming smile.

Hmm.

I'd been smiling about the *luscious locks* comment, but that clue into his behavior, the self-effacing remarks, had an awareness trickling through me.

It also had my lips parting.

"I have anxiety."

"What, honey?" he asked.

"I have anxiety," I said. "Sometimes I'm fine, but most of the time I'm not. It like...gets me in its grip and clamps down so tightly that sometimes I can't breathe or talk. People will look at me, expecting an answer, waiting impatiently, and I can't—" Air shuddered out of my lungs. "I want to reply or say something witty and *I can't.*"

I froze.

That wasn't what I'd been expecting to say, wasn't something I often admitted to *anyone.* It was my shameful, pathetic secret, something I'd worked to hide for so long, something I'd been *pressured* to hide.

And now it was just out there.

Kind of like Smitty had put himself out there.

"Baby," he whispered.

The endearment slid through me, roughened fingertips on my cheek, along my throat, dipping between my breasts.

My anxiety ramped.

"I can't do this," I whispered back.

His brows drew together.

"I know you think, like, you and me and"—I broke off, gestured between the two of us, eyes dipping to my hands—"b-but I can't do that."

"Hey." His voice was gentle.

"I try," I said softly. "I've worked so hard to get better and to not be like this, but...I am. There's something wrong with me inside."

He inhaled sharply.

And then he was on his knees in front of me, his big hands wrapping around mine. "There is absolutely *nothing* wrong with you."

It was said in his big, fierce way, the expression on his face so intense that I could do nothing but sit there and listen to him, to let his words wash over me.

"Nothing," he repeated.

"If there's nothing wrong with me," I said, my voice wobbling at first before it stabilized, before it got strong, like I was trying to be, "then there's nothing wrong with you."

He went still.

Hands tightening, just slightly, around mine.

And then he leaned forward—just forward and not *up* because he was so much bigger than me, so that when I was sitting and he was kneeling, our faces were aligned.

Our *mouths* were aligned.

Hot breath on my lips.

His nose brushing mine.

Closer.

Then his head tilted, his mouth hit my cheek.

"Thank you, sweetheart."

NINE

Smitty

A SHARP BREATH IN, her lips parted and tempting, even more so when her tongue darted out, moistened the bottom one.

Progress.

Words that were rattling around my head, about me, about her.

Clarity.

And...*yeah* progress.

It wasn't that she didn't like me, or at least, I didn't think so, considering I was kneeling in front of her, holding her hands, and she wasn't running for the hills.

But...she'd just given me something big.

And as much as I wanted to kiss her, I couldn't.

Not right then.

I sucked in a breath, released her hands, and slowly moved back into my chair.

Kailey blinked, those green eyes shuttering for a moment, and I held my breath, wondering if she would backtrack.

But then her chin came up, just slightly, and she nodded at my laptop. "So, do you want help?"

"THERE," she said, clicking the final selection. "All done." Surprisingly—or maybe not considering her specialty—Kailey was a control freak when it came to the tech...and the trackpad.

I hadn't needed her to click the responses I'd selected, but her doing that *had* required me to lean close to see the screen when she'd insisted on being the one to do the clicking.

Which had led to *my* leaning in.

Which had then been followed by her *not* leaning away.

More progress.

Especially because I wouldn't have expected her to demand anything from me, and the fact that she *had*...yeah, I was definitely feeling that progress.

And surprisingly, I hadn't minded when she'd begun skimming ahead and reading to me—which outside of an audiobook, was something I'd hated growing up. I already felt stupid a good sixty percent of the time, so having someone emphasize that by blazing by me in reading speed and then having the audacity to just do it so easily always stung.

But there was no condescension in her voice.

Just a husky rasp that slid over my skin like lace, which made me want to forget the promise to just be friends that I'd made all of an hour before.

Did I want more?

Fuck yeah.

Was I going to respect her boundary? Also, *fuck yeah* (albeit that *fuck yeah* was slightly less enthusiastic).

She hit submit, rolled her shoulders, and my gaze was drawn to the slender column of her throat, the way her blouse clung to the curves of her breasts.

My cock twitched and I reached for the laptop, needing the cover.

"Wait," she began, "you have to close it proper—"

I shut the top, dropped it onto my lap, the heat from the computer probably frying my sperm, but what the fuck did I need that for now? The only woman my dick had shown the least amount of interest in in *months* was Kailey, and she wasn't going to jump in bed with me and—

"—ly," she finished, and I couldn't help it.

The juxtaposition of my thoughts—sexy body to fried sperm—was too much.

I laughed, loudly, cutting myself off when she jumped. "Sorry."

She reached out, hesitated, then lightly patted my arm. "Don't be." A whisper. "Just...be you.

"So, here are some resources for your personality type," Hazel said, handing me a stack of papers. "I know it looks like a lot." A smile. "But there's a page with all the big bullet points, and the rest of it is just in case you want to learn more."

I took the pages, glanced at them long enough to see that there were five characteristics in bold, to focus and read the words.

Then I set them aside and picked up the ball I always played with during these meetings.

And insert *all* the balls and playing with them jokes here.

Hazel's gaze went to my hands, to that ball, and she grinned, though if I had to guess, I'd say her thoughts were less about my testicles and more about the fact that she always liked to tease the guys about not being able to sit still during her sessions with us. That's why she had the bucket of foam balls and the punching bag, the mini basketball hoop in the corner.

"So," she said. "I'm guessing that you're wondering why you get a dissertation on personality traits and what the hell that has to do with hockey."

"I mean," I grumbled, tossing the ball and…swoosh! Nothing but net. "I mean, I get homework and Marcel got to break shit."

Hazel got quiet, and I turned to see her looking thoughtful.

"And you think breaking shit is more in your wheelhouse than his?"

Uh-oh.

Danger lay down that path.

I shrugged, moved to shag down the ball. "I'm big and strong, and it's fun breaking shit. *That's* what I'm saying."

Silence.

Then, "Hmm."

Then she asked me about my family and my childhood.

That thoughtful look remained in place. "And your brother? Was he happy that you made it into the league?"

I paused, surprised by the question. "Yeah, of course. My family's been really supportive."

She tilted her head, studying me closely. "Your brother used to play, right?"

"I—" I frowned. "Yeah, but he hasn't for years." I scrubbed a hand through my beard. "Maybe since he was a teenager."

"Did you break things then?"

The ball I'd been tossing hit the carpet. "What?"

"You say you're best at breaking things and hitting guys. I'm just wondering if that's how you've always played or if it's something that's evolved over the years."

"I..." I picked up the ball. "Well, I wasn't as big of a guy then. I used to play, or"—a shrug—"at least, I used to think that I was a bit like Marcel. Smooth and fast, good hands. Then, my coach...well, we decided that I was better suited for defense."

She frowned.

"It's not like it seems. I was just...a disappointment—" Fuck. Why had I said it like that? Now her expression was concerned, and she was looking at me like...*fuck*, like I was a little bit pathetic. "I just...I had a better chance of moving forward as defense. The position came more naturally and I love it. I really do. Protecting Marty. Being able to jump up in the play occasionally. But I really like working my ass off for the guys. *That's* my comfort zone, and though I missed the excitement of being the one who was getting all the glitz and attention at first." I grinned at her. "We aren't professionals because we're not competitive." She smiled back. "I'm glad I found my way back to the blue line. If my coach hadn't suggested"—ordered, really, but coaches didn't do anything else, did they?—"then I wouldn't be here, glitz or otherwise."

Hazel leaned back in her chair, her expression gentle, but not giving anything else away as she studied me.

And for some reason, I was...tense.

Was she judging me?

Had I said the right thing?

Would she think I was a disappointment, too? That I wouldn't fit with the team and—

Her lips curved. "I could see you with some glitz," she teased. "Glitter in that beard? A sparkly bowtie to go with all the plaid?"

Laughter bubbled up in my chest, and I tossed the ball, sending it sailing through the hoop. "I could totally rock some glitter and sparkles."

<hr>

THE *CRACK* OF MY STICK.

The cool air on my cheeks seeping in through my beard.

Long, flowing locks...on my face.

Heh.

I wondered if Kailey liked beards.

Maybe I should trim it up, try to look a little more put together. Maybe if I cleaned up decently, she would—

"Ow!" I cried, leaning forward and bracing against the sting of a puck hitting me right between the shoulder blades. I sucked in a breath, whipped around to glare at Theo. The bastard was looking suspiciously innocent.

But being as I had been part of plenty of mischief, I knew when someone was up to no good.

"What?" Theo asked, skating over, and snagging a puck.

Another puck.

The first being the one that had beaned me right between the shoulder blades.

"I'm so glad that we're on opposite teams for the scrimmage," I said.

And yeah, my tone was more than a little evil, and Theo went a little pale, but the skinny little fucker needed to understand to not fuck with me.

I was the one who did the fucking—

And *also,* yeah, that wasn't going to be a thought I uttered aloud.

Ever.

A whistle trilled, and I glanced up to see Tommy Franklin gesturing us over. Tommy was a former NHL player and had been the Breakers' head coach for a number of years. I was noncommittal about him and the job he was doing as a coach, but since I mostly worked with Jacob Ralston, the D coach—

also a former player—who had a sharp mind, was funny as hell, and *hadn't* been there, standing by and doing fucking nothing when Mark Fucking Shelby had been tearing the team apart piece by piece a couple of seasons ago, I could remain fairly neutral about the man who *had* been there while Shelby was spewing his poison.

Poison that had eventually ended Oliver's career, lost him his leg, and had fucked with every player on the roster, including Marcel.

Who was one of the coolest people I knew.

So, yeah.

Tommy Franklin wasn't one of his favorite people, but he was a decent coach. Even though he knew his stuff, he didn't try to play the big man and didn't scream just for screaming's sake. But I had lost some respect, frankly (no pun intended, despite my love of puns), when Tommy hadn't recognized what Shelby was doing to the room.

Luc, our GM, on the other hand, had taken ownership, apologized, then had taken actions to make sure the room never got that toxic again.

But moving on, doing the shit I loved to do—skating fast and hitting things (hitting *people*).

I followed my teammates over to the huddle, listened to Tommy's spiel, and then when we were dismissed to drills, I bided my time.

I worked hard, as always.

I focused, as always.

I learned, as always.

And then when it was time to scrimmage, I made sure that I got Theo back for the puck between the shoulder blades.

Tenfold.

TEN

Kailey

I WAS in my office when a knock came at the open door.

And, oh wow, my heart skipped a beat when I looked up and saw it was Smitty.

His hair was wet and slicked back, his wild beard appearing to have been given only the barest modicum of taming by his fingers. His big body was encased in a tight navy Dri-Fit top, his bottom half in gray sweats that...well, should have been illegal.

Or maybe that was my thoughts—

Big dick.

He had a big ole' dick.

It swayed in the confines of those gray sweats, less *confined* than highlighted, and it was nearly impossible to pull my gaze up, to *not* stare at that big ol' disco dick and want it in my mouth—

Oh, Lord.

I should *not* have read that spicy book that Hazel had

suggested to me the other night before my friend's wife—and okay, my *friend*—had passed out on the couch.

My friend.

Hazel was my friend.

Along with Oliver.

And I knew I could have more of them if only...I could *fucking talk to people!*

Well, I was imagining a big ol' dick in my mouth, so that had to be some measure of progress, right?

The dick stopped swinging, and...my gaze flew up, hit his, saw that there were flames of desire in his eyes.

"Um..."

My gaze dropped again, saw that there was a little—no, *a lot* —of action happening beneath his sweats, and...my mouth went dry.

What was happening to me?

Smitty cleared his throat.

He actually had to *clear his throat.*

This time my eyes flew up and stayed up and right, holy shit, I'd been caught looking at a coworker's dick. And yeah, were we only sort of coworkers because I just did some basic computer work and he, meanwhile, was part of the group of players who did the important stuff (like actually play hockey for the professional hockey team)?

Still, there was probably something against fraternizing with my coworkers, especially when that fraternizing came with dick-staring.

Right.

A breath.

Since I was unable to hold those deep brown eyes but couldn't allow my gaze to drift south to his dick *again*, instead, I allowed my gaze to drift to the thick black beard lining his jaw. I wouldn't have thought I could appreciate facial hair, not when I imagined it was scratchy and sort of icky—like, didn't it hold crumbs and shit?

But his looked big and thick, and it elicited thoughts of where else he was big and thick and—

Shit, my eyes were drifting down again.

"Are you…?" He trailed off, cleared his throat. "Is this too much? I mean, me being here?"

"No!" I hurried to say, and it wasn't.

In fact, since we'd talked and I'd sat next to him, helping him complete that personality quiz, comparing his answers to the ones I would make—and finding that the majority of the answers he'd chosen would be the ones—that knot in my belly that usually tangled itself further and grew and grew and *grew* until it seemed to be swallowing me from the inside out the longer I spoke with someone wasn't there.

It wasn't gone.

Not by a long shot.

I'd gone to my office, struggled my way through a meeting with Luc and then one with several members of the coaching staff and the statistician, and it had been present the entire time.

Knotting and twisting, filling the back of my throat.

Making it a challenge for me to push through and be a valuable member of the team. Luckily, talking about my program and its functions was a little easier than small talk or well, any other kind of talk.

It's why it had been easier with Oliver, even when we'd first begun chatting online.

A common interest.

Something I knew down to the very bones of my being.

I knew it so well that I didn't really have to think about what came next. It was…well, not easy, but it was something I could do *easily* enough that it didn't turn me into a giant ball of exposed nerves with a tongue that didn't work with whatever words did manage to escape that useless muscle in my mouth not making a lick of sense.

It just...wasn't twisting me into knots.

I'd seen a glimpse of his vulnerable underbelly, and he'd given it without preamble, and...hell, I had to respect him for that.

Had to *like* him for that.

Which...presented a multitude of problems.

How could I *like* him?

Besides the whole sexy lumberjack thing he had going with the plaid suit and the thick beard and the big dick swinging in his pants, it was that vulnerability and willingness to show it that had me wanting to know him better.

"Kay?"

"Hmm?" I asked.

Warm hands came in contact with mine, making me jolt and jump as his hot, calloused fingers wrapped around mine. "Do you want me to go?" he asked. "Is this too much?"

It was...and it wasn't.

"No," I whispered.

His beard twitched and I allowed my gaze to drift higher, and it was to see a flash of white teeth. "Is it my beard you're admiring then?" he asked lightly. "Because I know I can grow an impressive one."

Only he would describe his beard as impressive.

And that made my lips curve.

"You're ridiculous," I said softly.

Another flash of white. "I'm good at being ridiculous."

Now, what did that mean?

I had no clue, but a part of me—the little pieces inside me that were knot-free, had always remained knot-free—really didn't like that.

Because it was denigrating.

And Smitty was a good man.

"Fire."

"What?" My brows pulled together.

He released one hand, brushed his thumb beneath one of my bottom lashes and then the other. "Tell me, little bird, what's made that fire appear in your eyes."

"You," I whispered. "It's your fault."

His body rocked back like I'd dealt him an actual physical blow. "Me?" Concern deepening lines outside his mouth, at the corners of his eyes, in a collection of ripples on his forehead. "I'm the reason you look the way you do?"

"I—" I swallowed, because he was totally the reason for all the feelings rippling through me, and it was also totally *not* his fault. Everything was in my head, all twisting around. Only, words of explanation didn't come.

How did I say that I could talk to him when I couldn't talk to anyone else?

How did I explain this...connection, this...tie drawing me to him?

How did I tell him that I didn't like him denigrating himself because he was good and smart and funny and kind?

How did I give him all that when I was a mess who could barely hold a conversation?

I needed to figure out my own shit and my own life and my own anxiety. I needed to be normal before I thought of pursuing anything with a man. Because, yeah, he'd said he wanted to be friends, but he'd also made his interest clear. If I gave him an opening, he'd take it.

And he'd be disappointed when he got to know me, *really* got to know me.

Oh, he'd be nice about it when he left.

Because he was Smitty.

And he was a good man.

But when he broke things off—as men always did after getting through my walls—I would be just a little bit more broken, a little bit more shattered, a little bit more impossible to find my way back to whole.

Trust me, Kailey.

Believe in us.

Let me in, honey.

I had.

Three times.

With three men, who'd pursued me with a sort of dogged challenge, as though my shyness were a tactic to draw them in. My anxiety a tool to attract them. Playing hard to get when really, the words just wouldn't come.

They'd played the long game.

Once in high school, and I'd ended up having a panic attack when I'd lost my virginity.

Once three years later, in college, my therapist encouraged me to broaden my horizons, and I'd made it through the sex without panicking, but that not panicking was the best thing I could say about the entire experience.

And, eight months before, when a man had approached me at a restaurant and asked me out, I'd accepted, thinking that I'd read enough romance novels, bought and practiced with enough toys, masturbated enough times that I would be comfortable knowing how to enjoy the process...and...it had been fine.

Fine enough that we'd gone on a couple of dates, and I'd told him a little about me. Fine enough even though I'd never gotten *off*—for the record—though I thought that perhaps I'd done a decent job of pretending I had.

But then I'd had a moment. A moment where my anxiety had gotten the better of me, after a bad day at work, after a phone call from my father, and though I'd gotten that gripping panic under control relatively quickly, using my techniques from my therapist, he'd still seen it.

He'd played it cool.

Told me it was no big deal.

And he'd fucked me that night.

Then he hadn't called.

And I hadn't cared.

Not really.

Okay, I'd cared because...

Dammit.

I'd tried to be myself—well, the best version of myself—and when a little bit of the real me had squeaked out on the date, he'd...

He'd been happy enough to use me as a vessel to get off, but the glimpse inside was too much.

I wasn't enough.

I was a disappointment.

And...hell, I knew that I already liked Smitty too much, that if he looked inside and found me lacking...

That would break me...break me in a way that was permanent.

He dropped my other hand, stepped back. "I should leave you to your work."

I should let him go.

But when he turned to leave, I found I couldn't.

My arm shot forward, hand gripping his wrist. "No."

Slowly, he spun back to face me.

"No," I said again. "Don't go. I—I—I—" A breath, frustration making my grip tighten, my nails digging into his arm. I tried to get my fingers to unlock, not wanting to hurt him. But instead, he lifted a hand, dropped his palm over the top of my hand, and held me in place.

"I'm here," he said.

"It's your fault," I blurted.

His throat worked, but he didn't try to pull away again.

And fuck, God. Could I say any fucking thing right?

"I know," he whispered.

"You make me want something I shouldn't."

"I just..." A breath that lifted and dropped his big shoulders. "I just want to be friends, little bird. No pressure. Nothing except getting to know each other."

"Why?"

His brows drew together. "Why what?"

"Why would you possibly want that? We hardly know each other and—"

His hand on mine squeezed. "I saw you, and I knew."

"Knew what?"

"That you were someone worth knowing."

A punch to the gut. Those words were a punch to the gut. Not a disappointment. Not something to be ashamed of.

"How?"

He gently brushed the skin beneath my eyes again.

"These." I inhaled sharply. "I saw these—just for a second —and I felt it"—he thumped a fist to his chest, just above his heart—"*here*. I knew I needed to know you." His lips twitched. "Even though you wanted nothing to do with me."

"I—" That was the second time he called me *little bird*, but it wasn't the most important thing in that moment. It was...

I leaned back enough to meet his eyes.

"But how?" I asked. "I mean, I ignored you and barely said anything—"

"You *said, Not interested.*" His lips twitched again.

My cheeks went hot. "I'm sorry. I—" I bit the corner of my mouth. "I just—"

"Wasn't interested." He grinned. "Which was cool then. And it's cool now. You don't have to like me."

He thought I wasn't interested in him?

Him and his lovely smile and big dick and the beard I wanted to feel on my face?

Well, on my face and other places.

Between my thighs. On my breasts.

But I digressed.

Because the problem wasn't that I didn't like him. It was that I liked him too much.

He was dangerous and would make me want things and I would inevitably disappoint him and…

He was sweet and nice and gorgeous and strong and—

Ballsy.

Smitty just laid his feelings and thoughts and vulnerabilities out there. He was himself without apology and just took the shit that was tossed his way.

And he'd taken one look at me and knew that he wanted to know me?

Him?

Conner Smith.

How did that even make sense?

It didn't.

But it *did* make me want to be more. To be like him.

To be *ballsy.*

Which was probably why I did what I did next.

ELEVEN

Smitty

ONE SECOND, I was glancing down at her face, trying to discern the sparks in her eyes.

The next, I was seeing her face draw nearer.

"What are you—?" I asked.

Her nails dug in a little deeper, but it wasn't to hurt me, to push me away.

It was...

To lift her higher, high enough for her to get her other hand on top of my shoulder and—

"What are you doing, little bird?" I asked, though this time my question came in a whisper.

And *this* time I barely got the question out before she was huffing out a breath, that glimpse of fire reappearing, and those sparks were beautiful in her emerald eyes.

"What am I doing? What am *I* doing?" Her mouth pressed flat. "What I'm doing is trying to kiss you here," she snapped.

She *snapped*.

With fire in her eyes and pink on her cheeks and her plump, pink lips glistening and begging for my touch.

And because I was Smitty, because I was *myself*, I couldn't resist teasing. "I thought we were working on just being friends?" I tilted my head to the side, studying her face, ignoring my cock twitching in my sweats, the urge to take those pretty lips.

A glare.

An actual *glare*.

Since when did a woman glaring at me feel like an actual victory?

Since it was *this* woman.

Since it was this woman who was so fucking beautiful and intriguing and smart and soft and quiet and...*fiery*—

She dropped back onto her heels.

Wait. *Shit.* That wasn't what I wanted.

I wanted her on her toes, in my arms, pressed to me.

I wanted her naked and on that desk. I wanted to be on my knees between those bare legs, my mouth buried in her pussy.

I wanted—

Her not to step out of the circle of my arms, to not pull away.

So, I stopped her.

One hand on her hip, drawing her close. The other diving into her hair, tilting her head back. "Come on, little bird. Come on up and kiss me."

She froze, cheeks going pink.

But her eyes, her eyes remained narrowed. "No," she said tartly. "You had your chance and—"

Fuck it.

I'd kiss *her*.

Fingers threaded into the silk of her hair. My hand sliding so that my arm could band around her waist. Lifting her up—

and fuck, but she weighed nothing at all—drawing her even nearer, until her face was aligned with mine, her mouth...right *there...*

Hot breath.

Parted lips.

She smelled like cinnamon and coffee.

Her skin looked like velvet under the bright lighting overhead, and she was beautiful even though I'd heard the fluorescent bulbs described as harsh more than a handful of times.

"Smitty," she breathed. "We shouldn't..."

"Why?" I asked, rubbing my nose along hers, dragging it down, inhaling deeply on the skin of her throat. Cinnamon here, too. And flowers. And the barest hint of coffee. But mostly flowers, and woman, and...Kailey. "You want to."

She shuddered, lips parting further, her breath hitting my temple. "Your beard is softer than I expected."

"I thought about shaving it," I whispered against her neck, pressing my mouth to the part where it met her shoulder.

Another shudder.

"Don't." Her hands lifted, weaving into my hair. "I like it."

No shaving.

Got it.

"Okay," I agreed, drawing my lips back along her throat, slowly up until I reached her jaw.

Lips? Or ear?

I went for her ear.

A slow trek along her slender jaw, finding a spot that made her shiver.

"That's—"

"What?" I asked softly into her ear.

"Nice," she said.

And maybe some might think simply *nice* was an insult, considering that what I felt was absolutely *not* nice, not in the fucking least. But her nails were biting into my scalp and her body was limp against mine, and—

Fuck it.

Time to take that mouth.

A heft had her up and forward, our faces aligned.

Her pulse was fluttering in her throat like a hummingbird's wings were trapped just beneath the surface. "Little bird," I whispered.

"I—"

I kissed her.

It was...there were no words that I could possibly utter to describe what I felt when our bodies connected, our tongues tangled, when I had her breath mixing with mine. I wanted to write a fucking sonnet to the stars and the moon and the sky. I wanted to burn this touch, this kiss onto my brain, a permanent memory that I'd never forget. I wanted to freeze time, or to be able to reverse it, able to relive this time and time again.

But time didn't freeze, and our brains and lungs eventually needed air.

I broke away, breathing heavily. "Fuck, little bird. Fucking hell."

Her nails were still in my scalp, sharp little points of pain that spiked my need, made me want to rip off her clothes and feast on her. Who gave a damn that anyone could walk into her office, could see us and—

Fuck.

I couldn't keep kissing her.

Couldn't get her naked.

We were at work.

She'd just barely begun to trust me.

But, fuck, I couldn't let her go, not quite yet. So, I held tight, and I inhaled deeply, and I slowed my breathing, and...I kept her as close as possible.

"I..." she began.

"I know," I said. "*That's* what I felt when I first saw you."

"That much?" A breath, her cheeks flushing when she glanced up at me. "I only felt..."

"Fear?" I asked.

A nod. "Fear, yeah, because you're gorgeous, and gorgeous men don't talk to me."

I chuckled. "I think I'll need to get your eyes checked. I'm pretty damned far away from gorgeous."

"What?" Her brows drew together, and that fire came back. She pushed at my chest. "Put me down." A beat, glare forming. "Now, Conner."

I obeyed, setting her lightly on her feet. "What's the matter?"

"You." A poke to my chest. "Why do you do that?"

"Do what?" I asked, and now it was time for my brows to do some drawing, yanking together and forming furrows in my forehead so deep that I could actually feel them. "Little bird," I said. "Do—"

"Why do you keep calling me that?" she asked, then promptly waved a hand away. "Never mind. It doesn't matter right now. You are beautiful and masculine and give me total lumbersexual vibes. I could not believe that you liked me enough to approach me that first day, that you thought I was attractive enough to pursue. And see?" she added when I felt the furrows on my forehead dig deeper. "You don't like it when I talk bad about myself, so don't do it either."

My heart began to pound. "Look. I'm just a normal guy who plays hockey and knows my role. I'm big. I'm strong. I'm funny. That's it, and that's enough for me," I said. "I promise. It's not talking shit about myself. I know I deserve to be here. I work hard to pull my weight with the guys and fulfill my role. But I'm not—"

"Funny and protective and sweet and caring? Smart even though you have challenges? Persistent in the face of those?"

Now my heart thudded, pounded against my rib cage. "Kailey," I began.

"You're all of those things."

Fuck.

This woman was going to undo me.

Her hands came to my face, and she kissed me hard and fast and just long enough so that I had a fucking tent in my pants.

"So just deal with the fact that I think you're fucking cool," she snapped.

I bit back a grin then tugged a strand of her hair. "So just deal with it?"

Dropping back onto her heels, she nodded (and let it be noted that the nod was also paired with a glare). "Yup." The P was a pop.

"And are you going to just deal with the fact that I want you?"

She rocked back slightly, eyes going a little wide. "I..." A breath, her shoulders straightening. "I can accept that you think you do."

"Kailey," I warned.

Her smile was tremulous. "Hey," she said softly, "I'm a work in progress, right? Consider it a win that I didn't deny it outright."

This time I couldn't hold back my grin. God, I liked her. "Okay."

"I'll take that win." A curl of wickedness crept through me, something she seemed to detect because she sighed, started to shake her head. "Don't say it."

"Say what?" My grin widened.

"Whatever is making you smile like that."

"What?" I feigned innocence. "I was just thinking that if you'd take that win, you'd take—"

She groaned, dropping her head back.

I pressed a kiss to that exposed throat, tilted my head so that I could whisper, "You'll take it all, little bird?"

Another shiver, her hands clenching into fists.

"Not promising anything," she murmured.

I leaned closer. "I am."

A soft moan that nearly undid me.

Hazed green eyes blinking up at me.

"I'll see you tomorrow?"

A nod.

My knuckles running down her throat, soft skin, curves that begged to be touched.

But...progress.

So much that day.

So...I brushed my lips over hers.

Then slowly backed away. "Bye, little bird."

TWELVE

Kailey

I'D PICKED up another romance.

And my friend from my nightstand drawer.

Because...

I couldn't stop thinking about the kiss in my office.

The *kisses*.

I'd spent the afternoon in a blur after Smitty had left, part of me wondering where in the fuck that woman had come from, and the rest of me a ball of exposed nerves—or *need* rather.

I'd gone from not wanting to date him, to thinking he was really fun and smart and sweet, to wanting him in my bed, to...

Wherever I was right then.

Mental relationship status:

It's complicated.

All the worries were still there—that he'd look and find me lacking, that I'd panic and ruin things, that I wouldn't be enough and that I'd eventually disappoint him.

But...he had some skeletons, too.

And he doubted himself.

And somehow that made my doubt slightly less intense? Or all-consuming? Or—

Maybe I was just a ball of lust that needed several really good orgasms and I'd get back to myself.

"Right," I whispered.

Slake that lust.

Read some naughty books and put all those dirty thoughts into fictional men, and pretty soon I'd be back firmly on the side of not wanting to fuck Conner Smith.

So that was why I was wrapped in my fluffy robe, skin pink from my bath, my vibrator—the good one with the special clit tapping and suction as well as the big ol' dick part because I was a fucking whore and did not give a damn. Well...either that or all my naughty books had brought inspiration and now I had a collection of toys that cost almost as much as a used car; and my own bed by myself was the one place I felt comfortable exploring.

I knew what I liked *here*.

I was comfortable with going that route *here*.

So, lots of different vibrators, each with its own purpose, and so, had I chosen this particular one because it reminded me of Smitty and the gray sweatpants show he'd given me earlier?

Yeah.

Was I spending extra time processing that this particular evening?

That would be a no.

Unless bringing myself to several orgasms with a dick I was pretending was Smitty's was considered *processing*.

Hell, who knew?

Maybe it was in the fucked-up world of my brain and—

"Not tonight, Kailey," I whispered, rolling my shoulders and concentrating on my breathing. No spiraling when I was feeling loose and relaxed after my bath. No panicking when it was just me and my vibrator and—I picked up my Kindle—my favorite fictional sex god.

"Right."

I turned on my TV.

And was that me turning it straight to a season of a certain baking show where the contestants had lovely, smart-sounding accents and they all supported each other while trying to win a crystal cake stand?

Maybe.

But it was also the perfect background sound to my…efforts.

Not too distracting. Something I'd watched a million times before (and not while I was getting off). No sudden loud explosions or songs.

Just sweet people baking sweet things and making the occasional irreverent pun.

Perfect masturbation material.

And perhaps when I finished, I'd finally learn how to make the perfect kouign amman.

Right.

Covers back. Lube out—not that I needed it considering I'd been in a perpetual state of wet since Smitty had kissed me in my office. Vibrator on and…oh fuck yeah…*in*. Dialing in the settings until my hips were rocking, my head digging back into my pillow, my eyes mere slits as I read my favorite scene in my favorite smutty book that I'd already had queued on my Kindle.

"You'll take it, and you'll like it."

That was the hero speaking, but I heard it in Smitty's voice.

"You'll take it all, little bird?"

My breath catching.

Time counting down on the TV.

My pleasure beginning to ramp up.

My clit was pulsing. My pussy clenching around the hard shaft of my vibrator, wishing it wasn't just a vibrator, wishing it was...Smitty.

That he was there.

It would be good if he were there. Not like the other times.

He would make it good.

I knew that somewhere deep inside.

Deep.

Heh.

My chuckle had the vibrator moving and suddenly, it was hitting just the right spot. I moaned, my spine arching, hips canting, working myself against the toy. The E-reader was forgotten as my heels dug into my mattress, one hand keeping the vibrator in place, the other coming to my breasts, cupping roughly before rolling my nipple between thumb and forefinger.

"Oh, God," I breathed.

Right there.

So close.

So *fucking* close.

So—

My phone began buzzing.

"No, no," I said, my attention being drawn roughly away from my pussy, my clit, the vibrator. I fumbled, hands full of toy...full of toy...and tittie and—

Releasing my breast, I tried to hit the button to silence the call, but missed, knocking my phone off the nightstand, dropping it onto my chest.

"Shit," I whispered, trying to keep the toy in place, so fucking close that I just needed...ten...more...seconds.

But the phone was still buzzing.

And my vibrator...my vibrator, slowly *wasn't.*

The perfect pressure quickly turned into not enough, into a desperate sprint to the finish line, all while my fucking cell phone continued to bounce and ring and *vibrate* on my chest.

"Shit. Fucking. *Hell,*" I hissed, reaching for the phone, intending to chuck it across the room.

Except—

Fucking *hell.*

my finger slipped, dragging across the screen, and... *answering the fucking call.*

Then as I was processing that, I fumbled my grip and promptly dropped it to the mattress, sending it skittering over the lump of blankets and just out of reach.

"Fuck, fuck, fuck," I breathed, rolling to my side and scrambling toward it, the vibrator still inside me, its battery dying its slow death, and seriously, why the fuck hadn't I charged it after the last time I'd used it and—

My fingers found the edges of my cell.

Thank God.

I leaned up, started to hit end.

But then I heard it, "Kailey? *Kailey?* Little bird, are you okay?"

I was fantasizing about his dick being inside me, and...he was on the fucking phone. And my only inane thought was— how had he gotten my number?

"Little bird," Smitty demanded, his voice piercing through the speaker. "Answer me or—"

Another scramble.

This one brought the phone up to my ear. "Hello? *Hello?*"

Was I out of breath? Yes. Was it partly because of the scramble, but mostly because of what was happening between my legs and the fact that Smitty's rumbling voice was now in my ears instead of my mind.

"Are you okay?" he asked, real concern in his tone.

Okay? Yes.

Sounding like I'd just finished running a half-fucking-marathon when the only thing I ever ran was a razor occasionally (and I meant *occasionally*) up my legs.

But I couldn't exactly admit that I'd been masturbating. To him, no less.

"I'm fine."

"You sound like you're having trouble breathing. Did I catch you in the middle of a workout?"

"No. *God* no."

Now I could hear the smile in his voice. "No workouts," he said softly.

"I—" I rolled to my back and my breath caught when the vibrator slid back into the perfect position.

"Kailey, honey, is this a bad time?"

It was the worst fucking time, and it was the best one.

Because now my vibrator's battery decided that it could make one more valiant effort at living...and that living was blaring to full, glorious life, the clit stimulator chugging to attention, pulsing against the bundle of nerves, the shaft inside me buzzing fiercely.

"I—" I bit back a moan.

"What's that noise?"

My breath caught. "I—" *Oh God.* "Nothing."

"It doesn't sound like nothing. It sounds..."

I bit my bottom lip, trying to find the strength to shut the toy off or pull it out or end the fucking call. But his voice was there, and I'd already been imagining it was him inside me, him touching me. My moan escaped.

Silence through the phone.

The baking show was in the judging portion of the first challenge.

My Kindle was bouncing against my shoulder.

The cell was pressed to my ear.

And my toy...had brought me right to the edge.

"Please, tell me that I'm not imagining you getting off while talking to me right now." The voice had gone straight from husky to a rasp, and it sent a shiver through me.

"I—" My head arched back.

"Can you still hear me?"

My breath caught, but I managed a sound that sounded remotely affirmative.

"Fuck," he gritted. "You *are.*"

I tried to summon the mental fortitude to lie, but I couldn't. All I could manage was to contain the moans that were rising in my chest, my throat.

"And you're close." His voice had gone liquid, boiling through me, its heat scorching me from the inside out. "Oh fuck, little bird, you're close, aren't you?"

No words. But I could only manage another of those affirmative sounds.

"Fuck, little bird." He groaned. "And you're thinking about me, thinking about the kiss in your office this afternoon, aren't you?"

"I—"

I broke off again.

And he kept talking.

"I know you are," he rasped, "because it's all I've been thinking about. Because I just got out of the shower after stroking myself until I came, your name on my tongue, pretending it was your fingers around my cock, that you were working me until I exploded, that you took me deep and swallowed me—"

I exploded.

The most powerful orgasm I'd ever experienced.

Waves of pleasure blew through me with the force of a nuke, pulsing and twisting along my nerves until my body went limp, the cell slipping down to the mattress, my legs dropping open wide.

Slowly, oh so slowly, I returned to myself.

To Smitty's rough voice talking to me.

"You took it, little bird, and you did good."

My breath caught.

"And I can't wait to see your face when you do that with me."

"I should go," I whispered.

"Don't hide from me now, Kailey," he murmured, "and don't think for a fucking second that I'm not imagining your face right now, wishing that I was there. Don't think that for a second I wasn't doing the same thing twenty minutes ago. When I said your name was on my tongue, that I was imagining your hand gripping me as you sucked me deep—"

My lungs hitched at the erotic image, another pulse of that all-encompassing pleasure flying through me.

"Don't think for a second that my cock isn't hard again, wishing that I could transport myself through the phone."

"I—" A breath. "I don't know what to say."

"Don't say anything," he replied easily. "Just lay there and enjoy the afterglow."

So, I did.

Until I summoned the energy to turn off my toy, to dislodge the Kindle digging into my shoulder.

"Do you want me to go?" Smitty asked then, his voice quiet and soft and languid.

"I..." I didn't know what I wanted. "I...no," I finally admitted.

A pause, and I could sense that the word had brought him pleasure.

And...I liked that.

Wanted to do more of it.

But then he said, his voice less sex god and more joking Smitty, "Are you really jerking it to *Great British Bake-Off*?"

And I decided that maybe I wouldn't mind bringing him a little *pain* as well.

THIRTEEN

Smitty

I STROLLED THROUGH THE HALLWAY, the package in my hand crinkling, barely able to hold my grin back.

I'd gotten up at the crack of dawn after staying up way too late talking to Kailey the night before.

After—I had to be real there—getting off the phone with her, the clock showing two in the morning, and unable to sleep, so whacking off for the second time that evening...something I'd done again that morning in the shower.

I was going to start chafing.

I didn't give a fuck.

Not after hearing her breathy moans on the phone, my name on her tongue.

Kailey had done that.

With me on the phone—which, okay, had been an accident, because she'd confessed later that she'd been trying to end the call, not pick it up. But I'd take that accident and imprint it on my *soul*.

Never forgetting that.

Ever.

And now I was definitely going to find a way to use that toy on her, to see her shatter as she came with it.

Now I was going to find a way to get her to come on my tongue, to watch her face as she fell apart and—

"Were you..." A pause that yanked me out of my thoughts. "Were you going to come in?"

I was going to come *inside* her and—

Fuck, man.

Pull it together.

I'd slept with plenty of women. This wasn't the time to stomp forward like an elephant in an antique store, rattling the wares and knocking shit over. This was finessing the forward momentum and—

Fuck.

What did I know about finesse?

I was brute force and no filter.

Which was probably why I jerked my head up, saw those gorgeous green eyes locked on me, the pink on her cheeks, and asked, "Do you blush like that when you come, too?"

Her mouth fell open.

That blush went from zero to seven million.

The pencil she'd been holding dropped to the desk.

I strolled in, crossing to her, wondering what she'd do next. Tell me—probably rightfully—to get the fuck out. Invite me to come closer and demonstrate her ability to come (oh, please, God, let it be the second).

Her lips parted—

I braced, waiting.

"What's in the bag?"

I froze for a minute, my dirty mind already well down the path of her demanding I slam the door and telling me to get on my knees between her legs. Then I managed to reverse slightly, enough to process the question, remember the bag, and... "Here." I thrust it at her. "I..." Now *my* cheeks actually felt a little hot, though thankfully, my beard mostly covered them. "I got this for you after last night."

More pink flaring.

But, to her credit, she didn't back down.

Just grabbed the bag, opened it, and...

"You're such an ass."

But it was said with twitching lips as she pulled out the cookbook by one of the contestants from the show she had been watching the night before.

"For the next time you...get some inspiration."

A sigh and a smile and a shake of her head.

The Classic Smitty response as my mom would say.

But then fire in green eyes. The exasperated smile turning sinful. "Did you?" she asked, setting the book down and drifting closer.

"Did I what?" I asked, trailing my fingers through the ends of her hair, smelling the soft notes of flowers in the locks, the cinnamon on her breath and her skin, studying the spray of freckles that danced over her pert nose.

"Did you"—she rose on tiptoe, leaned up to whisper in my ear—"*find...inspiration?*"

I jumped when she flicked out her tongue.

And she dropped back onto her heels, smirking liked she'd won.

But since I could take it as well as I dished it out, I wrapped an arm around her waist, drew her flush to me, and said, "I did, little bird. Three times." A nip to the corner of her jaw. "Once before I called you. Once after we hung up." I flexed my hips lightly, just enough for her to feel that I was ready to *find inspiration* again. "And once more this morning, just before I went out to buy that."

A shudder skating through her frame. "Why?" she whispered.

"Mmm?" I inhaled the scent of her, drawing it deep into my lungs. "Why what?"

"Why did you get the book?"

I pressed my lips to her throat and then straightened, letting a little distance come between us. "Because I like teasing you."

Her brows drew together. "Why?"

I brushed a thumb beneath one eye then the other. "Because these shoot sparks at me."

The lines on her forehead deepened. "You want me to be annoyed with you?"

Yeah. I did. "Yeah, little bird, because you being annoyed with me means that you're not anxious around me, that you're seeing me, the real, annoying *me*"—more sparks that had me grinning, had her swatting me lightly on the chest—"and you're not in your head, not full of worry. You're here, in this moment, with me."

"I—" She paused for a long minute, seeming to consider that. Then her hand pressed to the spot over my heart, the one that was thudding away steadily, waiting for her verdict on that, hoping it was true, hoping that she'd agree with me. "You're right," she whispered. "I...am comfortable with you. I don't know why," she added, and I grinned at the perplexity that joined her expression. "By all accounts, I shouldn't be."

"It's because we're meant to be together," I said, matter-of-factly.

Her eyes went wide. "Um...what?"

"Yup." Inside, my heart was pounding, but outside I tried to play it cool...or as cool as I ever did. "I saw you and I knew. Some part of you knows that now."

"I..." She turned away, pushed her hand through her hair. "You know that sounds absolutely insane, right?"

"I do," I agreed.

Her gaze slid over her shoulder. "Right. So..."

A shrug. "It doesn't change what's in here." I pressed my fist to the spot over my heart. "This knows. It just...takes some time for the rest of it to catch up."

Her fingers played along the edge of the cookbook. "And what if it doesn't?"

I knew that wasn't going to happen. The heat. The kiss. The phone call. Her being comfortable with me.

I'd known this woman was it for me from the moment I'd laid eyes on her.

I'd make sure it happened.

But this wasn't the time for pressure.

Because the fire in her eyes had been tamped out. I'd gone too big, too fast, too *Smitty*. So, I shrugged. "Then the rest of it won't, and we'll just be friends, yeah?"

"I—" Her lips pressed flat, a frown deepening into lines surrounding her mouth. "Smitty, that's not so simple—"

A knock at the door.

Oliver stood there, his tablet in one hand.

He glanced from Kailey to me and his brows lifted. "I can come back..."

Maybe I should have hated my friend for the interruption, but frankly, it had come at the perfect moment.

Get her distracted, off the topic of what I knew was an inevitability in my heart, what I needed to convince her of, even if that convincing wasn't going to happen at that moment.

This would buy me some additional time to get her there.

Or rather for me to regroup and find the right moment to circle back and reapproach.

Hopefully, with more finesse.

Or at least, with slightly less Smitty.

Oliver gestured down the hall. "I'll just—"

"No," I said. "Don't let me interrupt your meeting. I need to get on the ice anyway."

Oliver's eyes were on mine, warning and curiosity mixing in the pale blue depths. "Smitty."

"See ya," I muttered.

"*Smitty,*" Oliver hissed.

"Later."

Then I was vapor—

Or at least, a six-foot-something hockey player who was hauling ass down the hallway.

Same difference anyway.

FOURTEEN

Kailey

OLIVER LIFTED A BROW.

I felt my cheeks get hot, the tell-tale twisting beginning in my belly.

His face gentled as he moved forward, dropping into a chair, holding out his tablet so I could see the screen. "I was thinking..." he began.

And then he proceeded to throw a curveball at me that would require me to write a whole lot of code.

So basically, he pulled me right out of my head, and the swirling in my mind and gut and focused me on what calmed me—my work.

But it was only a temporary solution.

Because when I paused in my note-taking for what I'd do when he left me to my program and my code and the safety of the clarity of the coding language that ran my program and happened to look up at him, he was staring at me.

In concern.

"Smitty?" he asked.

I sucked in a breath, released it on a five-count, slowing the spinning.

He let me do that, didn't push further, and because it was Oliver—and also, maybe because it was about Smitty—the coil unwound. It relaxed.

It disappeared.

"He thinks we're meant for each other."

Oliver sat back in his chair, both brows lifting high. "Man doesn't mess around, does he?"

That had me chuckling, nerves creeping. "No, apparently not." I pushed back my bangs. "I mean, I know it's probably inappropriate or I should have checked with HR first." More nerves. "Shit, I mean, is there some sort of fraternizing paper-work I need to be filing? I—I—we only kissed once but last night—" I clamped my teeth together before I blurted out what had happened on the phone the previous evening, but my gaze caught on the cookbook, and I felt my cheeks flare.

"Kailey?"

"Yeah?" I asked, seizing the book and shoving it into my desk drawer.

"No one cares if you date Smitty."

My head shot up.

"So long as you're both consenting adults and stuff doesn't get weird if it doesn't work out," he said. "Then no one cares. Hell, Luc dates head counsel. I'm with Hazel. Marcel is with Pru, who's in charge of development. Consent. Happy. No drama at work, and everyone's cool, okay?"

Lungs feeling like they were in a vice, albeit one that was slowly releasing, I nodded. "Okay."

"Now," he said, lips beginning to turn up at the corners. "When are we going on a double date?"

A KNOCK at the door drew my gaze several hours later.

I'd been in full focus mode for ages, so glancing up and blinking at whoever was knocking was like stepping out into the bright sunshine, and it took a hot minute for my eyes and brain to focus.

On Hazel.

She held a bag.

"I hate to interrupt the flow," she said. "But it's well past lunch and Oliver mentioned that he'd given you something new to work on."

My brows pulled together.

Hazel smiled. "He also mentioned that you tend to be singularly focused when working on a new project." She jiggled the bag, the paper crinkling. "So, here's me singularly focusing you on a bit of sustenance before you get back into it."

My heart skipped a beat, and for a moment, I didn't know how to respond to that.

It was thoughtful.

And really sweet.

Both of which were quintessentially Hazel.

But I was hard-pressed to remember a time when *I'd* experienced thoughtful and sweet.

Sharp, sharp words. Tiptoeing through a kitchen. A smack to the side of the head. Hair being pulled.

That was reality.

Not *this*.

But *this* made me feel...warm and buoyant and—

Right. Time to stop staring at Hazel like an idiot.

"Wow," I managed. "I—*thanks*." I gestured at the chair in front of me. "Should I go to the vending machine and get us some drinks?"

Hazel grinned. "Oh no," she said as she sank into the seat, and there was a twinkle in her brown eyes.

What?

Okaaay...

Well, I didn't really need drinks anyway. I had a bottle of water.

Hazel leaned forward. "When we want drinks, we hit the boys' kitchen." A wink.

"So, I'll go to the kitchen then?" I asked.

A shake of Hazel's head. "In the future, yes." The affirmative paired with the head shake threw her. "Today," she went on, "you won't need to—"

Movement behind Hazel.

A big body, his freshly showered scent reaching my nose. Smitty held a bag, and this time I didn't think it contained a cookbook that would bring a blush to my cheeks. "I don't want to interrupt," he said softly and for some reason, this made Hazel's grin widen. "I just wanted to bring you this."

And...

He set two cans on the desk.

Along with two Smitty-palm-sized cookies beside them— which meant they were giant.

As I knew.

Since they'd been on my ass, in my hair, coasting along my side, cupping my jaw. The memories made me shiver, heat flowing through me.

Then I looked at one of the cans.

What *drink* it was.

A special type of sweet peach tea that I knew for a fact wasn't carried in the vending machines, and considering that the kitchen was home to healthy snacks and drinks courtesy of the nutrition staff, I highly doubted sugar-loaded sweet tea would be one of the offered options.

But there it was.

Sitting on my desk with beads of condensation starting to roll down the aluminum cylinder.

Along with two cookies.

My lips parted and I felt my eyes go wide, drifting from the can to Smitty and over to Hazel, who was wearing a shit-eating expression.

"Right," Smitty said, rocking back on his heels, looking so different from that morning, so unsure and out of place. "I'll leave you to your lunch, little bird," he murmured.

Uncertainty in the big man's frame, on his face.

I hated that.

So, I reached for his wrist, wound my fingers around it and squeezed. "Thank you," I whispered.

"I—" A hand through his beard then thrust through his hair, mussing the damp locks. "It's nothing," he said quietly.

Another squeeze, hoping that my eyes showed exactly how much it meant to me.

But though he nodded, that uncertainty didn't go away, not completely anyway.

Words.

He needed the words.

And though my insides were squeezing tight, throat full of tension, I managed to whisper, "It's not nothing to me."

The uncertainty flitted away.

A cocky smile took its place. He turned his arm, dislodging my grip on his wrist as he spun his hand, wrapped my fingers in his own. They were warm and strong and big...just like him. And, just like him, his hold on my hand settled me.

Like something deep inside me, beneath the roiling anxiety, the self-doubt, the scars that had hardened my protective shell, had unfurled.

Opened.

To him.

And only him.

My pulse sped, prickles on my nape, sweat between my fingers.

A furrow between my brows.

That he smoothed away with a gentle swipe of his thumb. "I know," he whispered. A wicked grin. "Think you'll be able to *take* the whole can."

Laughter—part cackle, part outraged mirth, part teenage-esque giggles—bubbled up in my chest.

Which he knew.

Because he nipped my bottom lip. "Call me while you're watching *Great British Bake-Off* later, yeah?"

Oh. I was so going to kill him.

Especially since my cheeks flared and Hazel looked intrigued and my thoughts went fully dirty—like seriously, he was so damned good as just a voice on the phone, how would he be in person, "watching" the episodes with me?

Which had a wicked thought pinging through my mind.

I crooked a finger, grinning when he bent so I could whisper in his ear. "Or maybe you should come over and we can watch together."

He straightened like I'd shocked him. "What?" he croaked.

And I supposed I had.

I'd kind of shocked myself.

Okay, I'd *really* shocked myself, and though some part of me—okay, *my clit*—had meant it, wanting that rough voice, those warm, strong hands on me, the rest of me couldn't believe I'd just uttered the invitation.

Smitty knew that.

Because his face stayed warm, but it also went soft, and he tugged lightly at a strand of my hair. "Soon, little bird, soon."

Warm and wicked.

Sweet and teasing.

I *liked* this man.

I liked who I could be with this man, liked that I could gather myself and lift my chin, fill my voice with tart, tell him, "We'll see," and we both knew it was an inevitability.

That he'd be in my bed, more than likely without the reality show blaring in the background.

He'd be there and his hands would be on me, his body over mine, his cock inside.

A bop to the tip of my nose. "Yeah," he said. "We'll see."

Then he was gone again, disappearing out into the hallway, leaving me alone with Hazel.

Who was fanning herself.

"Holy sexual tension, Batman," she said, tugging at the collar of her shirt.

I froze. "I—"

"How does it feel to be one of us now?" Hazel asked, opening the bag with aplomb and setting out our sandwiches. "Struck dumb by all that hockey masculinity until you forget that you're at work and want to jump their bones—or *bone*, rather"—a smirk—"and preferably, that bone-jumping will happen with you perched on your desk while they're orgasming you into oblivion and—"

"Is this your fantasy or mine?" I interjected.

And then felt my mouth drop open.

Where in the hell had that come from? Surely not my mouth since that was a level of snark I'd never managed aloud. On direct message, sure. But forming the words on my tongue and actually *saying* them? Not so much.

At least, I'd not been able to do it with anyone except Smitty.

I had snark for him.

Ever since we'd huddled around his laptop, and he'd opened up...and I'd shared and...

Certainty in my belly, spreading up and out.

Maybe he was right about our hearts knowing each other. Maybe—

Hazel burst out laughing. "Guilty," she said, unwrapping her sandwich and taking a big bite, talking around the veggies and cheese and meat. "I may have a desk fantasy." She smirked again. "Mostly because with Dominic at home, it's really hard to live *any* of my fantasies."

I blinked.

"Crap." Hazel rubbed her forehead. "I didn't mean it like that," she said quickly. "It's just...hard to be a mom and a sexual being. Especially, when I'm covered in spit-up and poop half the time."

"I can't say that I completely understand," I said. "But having been on the receiving end of Dominic's drooling powers, I can sympathize."

We both laughed this time, and I was able to do it because Smitty made it possible for me to understand teasing that didn't come from someplace mean. But it wasn't just him. Oliver had built that bridge and Hazel had helped pave it, but *Smitty* was the one who'd given me the courage to cross it. I could be myself, and I could interact with my friends—

Hell, I was *worthy* of friends and positive attention.

And maybe that wasn't something that was all that amazing and out there.

Most people were probably born with that understanding, had it fostered by family and teachers and coaches.

But mine had been crushed to powder, washed away.

Until Oliver had invited me here to join the organization.

And Hazel had welcomed me in hers and Oliver's and Dominic's lives.

Until the team had included me in their events.

Until…a six-foot-plus man with a lumberjack beard and a penchant for plaid had shown kindness. He'd kissed me like a thunderstorm on a hot summer night, the sticky air clinging to my bare skin, the breeze coasting through my hair.

And given me a can of tea.

Then had flayed himself open and accepted my vulnerability with the same amount of openness he'd given me.

Add a dash of patience, plenty of wicked, and how he looked at me and *saw* me and liked *me,* and somehow only found himself lacking. *Him.* Not *me.*

It was unfathomable.

But it was a truth I was finally understanding.

One that meant I could keep moving forward.

Inching toward the person I wanted to be while accepting that the person I was right at that moment was just as good.

I had the strength to keep moving, to keep swimming, to keep making progress—even crawling if I had to.

But I was finally out of that rigid prison.

Worthy and good and…not a disappointment.

There was laughter in Hazel's eyes. Not disappointment.

And when I looked deep into myself, for the first time ever, I didn't find disappointment either.

FIFTEEN

Smitty

A WHISTLE.

The crowd quieting.

Hockey.

Fuck yeah.

A real game. No more of this preseason with half the roster of rookies bullshit. This was the real game. The first *real* game of the season.

And the crowd in our home arena was *lit*.

Sold out.

A sea of blue and black and white.

None of our opponents' colors—or at least none that could be spotted with the naked eye. And I wasn't really looking at the crowd, anyway. My focus was on the team box overhead, and the silhouettes I could deduce down from ice level, the occasional shots of the people inside on the Jumbotron.

Okay, I wasn't looking at people.

I was looking at *Kailey*.

We'd talked on the phone the night before—unfortunately, sans baking show, and unfortunately a fairly short conversation because she'd been working.

Which I hadn't liked at first.

She worked hard and deserved downtime.

But she'd answered the phone with distraction in her tone, and I couldn't miss the way she'd perked up when she realized it was me, how excited she'd gotten when she'd given a simple explanation about what she was doing, and I'd shown interest.

Had asked her a few simple questions, and she'd acted like it was the first time a man had shown genuine interest in her work.

Which begged the question of what kind of assholes she'd been dating.

Well, no more assholes.

I was hers now.

Of course, my questions had brought a slew of terms I hadn't known or understood, so I'd rushed to jot down the words I didn't know on an old receipt as she talked, googling them after we'd hung up, realizing that I had a lot to learn if I wanted to comprehend, at least a little bit, what her work was.

Something more than just she was good with computers and could make programs and stuff.

But the words had swam on the screen, and I hadn't gotten as far as I wanted, especially since my mind was focused on remembering the slight husk of her voice, the excitement in her tone that had reminded me of our baking show escapades, the soft sound that rose in the back of her throat when I kissed her.

So, I'd called it quits on the screen time.

Then had jerked off in the shower.

Yup.

I was *definitely* going to get chafed.

Luckily—albeit not for my chafing issue—we had a road

trip coming up. I'd have plenty of time to learn about coding while on the plane and in the hotel, so I'd spent the morning downloading some podcasts and audiobooks to supplement anything that would require me staring at a screen getting more and more frustrated that I couldn't read the words I wanted without struggling.

But...

That was my challenge.

Head down. Push through. Keep on grinding.

"Let's keep it clean, eh boys?"

I blinked, thankful for the ref's chatter when I realized that I was daydreaming about coding when I should be focused on making a good opening effort for the fans in the stands, and especially for Kailey, who I'd watched battle indecision when Oliver and Hazel had invited her to join in the box a few hours before.

Teeth into her bottom lip.

Her eyes skating along the hallway.

Then her shoulders straightening and her chin coming up and...

Agreement.

With a proud, triumphant smile I felt right in my belly.

And it was that proud, triumphant smile that I was going to use to motivate me—or motivate me more than the normal hockey excitement and home crowd and first *real fucking game* (!) of the season.

Good shit.

Awesome shit.

Spectacular—

The puck dropped.

My mind went immediately blank.

There weren't even hockey thoughts, no notions of plays to do, passes to make, hits to finish. I wasn't cognizant of what my feet were doing or the thousand little pieces of the game, the minutiae that I'd drilled into myself over and over again, until I didn't *have* to think.

Until it was just me on the ice.

Hockey in my blood and muscles and nerves and skin.

Hockey that was my life.

Hockey that—

The air wheezed out of me as a fucker from the other team slammed me into the boards, trying to jostle me off the puck, but I held tight to my stick, positioned my feet so the puck stayed between us, so I could slightly tilt one when Marcel came up and let my teammate scoop the rubber disc free, sweep it across the ice to Raph who began hauling ass up the right side.

Gaining the offensive zone, carrying it deep.

I was pushing off the boards, hustling after him, Marcel already thirty feet ahead, being an outlet for Raph as our opponent's defense and center closed in.

My heart was pounding. Sweat was already dripping down my temples.

Thirty seconds at a full speed NHL game and I was already tired.

But that was the game.

And that was why I worked out so hard.

Because I'd barely gotten close to the opposite blue line when Raph, Theo, and Marcel turned the puck over and I needed to get my ass back into my own zone, to protect Martin, our goalie.

Three on two, with me and Cas the only two Breakers back, Washington's top line closing in on us.

A pass.

I cut the angle preventing the second from coming across the middle.

Out of the corner of my eye, I saw our top forward trying to streak toward the net. Luckily, Marcel was skating back as fast as he'd flown up, Theo and Raph right on his heels.

We'd have numbers soon.

And the bigger threat was that backdoor pass behind Martin.

So, I shifted position, split the difference, held my breath, and when that pass to the back door sailed, I dove forward, knocking it into the corner and out of danger.

Lungs burning, I hopped to my feet, skated after it.

Returned the favor of that breath-stealing hit into the glass.

The crowd roared.

Marcel cleaned up the puck, got it to Theo, and he cleared it down.

Then it was time to change.

Full speed to the bench, pushing through the door as the next line hopped over the boards.

My eyes hit the Jumbotron. Forty-seven seconds since the puck had dropped.

And I was dripping with sweat, lungs sawing. Though already I was drinking water infused with a bit of Gatorade, swapping my wet gloves out for dry ones from the equipment guys, sucking in air and ready to go by the time the other three D pairs cycled through.

Hopping on the ice.

More skating. More hits. More passes and chasing down pucks and protecting Martin.

A red light flashing and a cheer rising in my chest—and in the stands—when Theo tapped a puck home off a pass from Marcel.

One buzzer to call the first period to an end. Another to signal the completion of the second.

A final one bringing the game to a close, our one-nothing

victory not one hundred percent the one we wanted (we always wanted to destroy our enemies), but it was one we'd take. Two points was two points and in a season with eighty-two games, we'd file away any victory we could.

Next time we'd bring the needed destruction.

For now, I was fist-bumping my teammates, accepting the pat on the back from my coaches, the light shove and grin from Raph when I was announced as the first star of the game—which basically meant that I had to take a skate around center ice and got to give a kid a signed puck then had to speak with the media on the way back to the showers.

I'd gotten the first star a couple of times.

It was no big deal, and I really liked making a kid smile—and really liked making the little boy with a big, toothy grin, a neon pink Breakers jersey paired with a bright blue beanie jump in joy when the adult near him caught the puck I had tossed over the glass and handed it over.

What could I say? Kid had style.

Also, I was glad the adult followed hockey etiquette and didn't try to pocket the puck.

Occasionally, there was an asshole who'd try to take the shit from the kids.

But this guy was cool, so I nodded at one of the ushers who'd been with the organization for years and who I had prepped for this scenario (they had agreed to carry a few items I paid for to give away at their discretion). The guy, Tom, nodded back and quietly handed the guy a hat.

Because the adults—the cool ones anyway—deserved something nice, too.

I didn't stay to see the guy's reaction.

I had a soundbite to give in the hall and then a longer interview for the post-game media circuit. There was more interest than normal since it was the first match-up of the season, so it took a while for me to get to the locker room, divest myself of my gear. Padding and protective equipment hung up or on the shelf of my cubby. Jersey and socks into the bins in the center of the room. Walking through to the shower area and heading for the training suite. I had a quick post-game I always did when I had time, a short bike ride, some time on my favorite foam roller.

I'd named her Ursula.

And she made me hurt in the best possible way.

Thighs and hips. The sides of my ribs. My back.

Twenty minutes later, the majority of the game's strain was gone, and Samantha, our head trainer, who'd come through the training suite, had given me an approving nod which I'd interpreted as appreciating my stretching and lack of injuries.

I'd see what happened as the season went by. Most of the time, injuries were inevitable. The wear-and-tear on the body during the season meant that there was always a risk, especially in the lead-up to the playoffs and the post-season.

Because we'd be in the post-season.

We'd be going for another Cup.

I wanted to heft it again, wanted to ensure that the Breakers became a fucking legacy.

So, I'd take the bumps and bruises and sore muscles and injuries.

Hockey was my life, what I'd lived and breathed for, what I'd dreamed of...what I was good at, and some might say, the *only* thing I was good at.

So, I stretched and rolled and when I was done, I went back through the shower area and into the private changing area, stripped down (the dirties going in another rolling bin) and headed for the showers.

Naked.

As was my way.

But the room had emptied out, only a few of the guys remaining.

Theo was pulling on his suit, Marcel and Raph had already hit the door. Cas was tying his shoes. Flynn and Walker and Jackson would all be dressed and out of there before I got done soaping up.

Fine with me.

Meant I'd get less shit about my post-game shower routine.

Which was...air drying.

My mouth quirked. That was better for the skin.

Shower on hot, bordering on scalding, just like I preferred. Steam filling the space, licking up at my calves and torso, condensation clinging to my beard. The stream was strong, and I dunked my head in, letting the water sluice over my body, sink into my tight muscles before I was remotely ready to get out.

But I needed to get home.

And maybe I'd text Kailey, see if she was still up and wanting to watch that baking show.

Grinning now with that thought, I finished with the shampoo and soap (and bit of conditioner, 'cause gotta keep that beard soft), wrenched off the water, shook myself to get the extra water, and then slung a towel around my shoulders as I strode into the locker room.

A few sighs, but I ignored them as I went around my air-drying, returning their goodbyes as they took off one-by-one.

The room went quiet.

And...I took my first full breath of the day.

No pressure. No more expectations. No more noise.

Just me and the room and—

A soft noise.

A flicker of movement at the door.

SIXTEEN

Kailey

I SHOULD HAVE GONE HOME a long time ago.

But I'd hung in the box talking with Oliver about the game (and his new dragon), Hazel checking in with their sitter a few times, but since Dominic was asleep, she'd wanted to enjoy the rare night out sans baby.

Then I'd drifted downstairs, running into a couple of the coaches and Pru, who was one of the main users of the program I had created.

Pru was...what I wanted to be when I grew up.

Strong and loud, confident and *ballsy*.

But she was soft, too. The way she melted into Marcel and how their bodies seemed to be in constant awareness of each other. Shifting and realigning so they fit together perfectly. Hazel and Oliver had that, too, along with Luc and Lexi.

It was beautiful, and I'd found myself being far more social now that I'd noticed it.

And the longer I was around , the longer that ball of nerves in my stomach, the one that was always there and the one that probably would never fully go away, had sunk deeper and deeper. But that was so much better than spinning faster and faster, the barbed edges of that tangled ball lashing out and cutting my insides to ribbons.

Maybe one day it would sink so deep that it would drop out of me completely.

Like laying an egg.

That had my lips twitching as I turned and walked toward the exit, but not before promising to call Marcel's dad, Leo, when I had a free moment to discuss some software he wanted created—me and Leo jived, mostly because he was as much of a geek as I was. But he was so much like Pru that it was hard to be anxious with him, not when he was talking a mile a minute about stuff I was comfortable with and never got impatient with my answers. He wanted to see if I wanted the side project or could recommend someone else.

Freelancing was my gaming and book money.

So, I'd probably be down.

Plus, it was good practice for me. There would be comfortable, positive interactions with little to no anxiety (because Marcel's dad was awesome), and I could keep building on those, continue growing and moving forward and—

I'd instinctively started moving forward, hurrying because I was coming to the hallway that would lead me right by the guys' changing room.

Always head down, no risk at seeing anything.

And plus, the outer door was always closed anyway.

Except today...not closed.

The blond wooden panel was pushed wide. The lights inside dimmed. The room empty—

A flicker of movement.

No.

Not empty.

My lips parted as a wave of heat hit me with the force of a tsunami.

Smitty was standing there.

Naked with only a towel around his neck. And, sweet baby dragon, I'd always discounted *big* men in the romance novels I read as something that fiction writers made up, and yeah, I'd caught a glimpse in those gray sweatpants, but it was fucking different seeing that cock out in the wild.

I went wet, could feel my panties clinging to my pussy. My nipples tightening, rubbing against my bra, the slight chafe a tease and not nearly enough.

Right.

I should…

Leave.

He might want privacy—except, hadn't I heard all those stories about him liking to parade around naked?

Maybe he liked people to watch?

Maybe he would like me—

Wait, Kailey. Jesus, I thought, slamming my eyes closed. *On the life of your dragon, Esmerelda, he hasn't consented to you staring at him like a creeper. Keep. On. Walking.*

Right.

This was wrong.

But my lids slit open, and I inhaled sharply at all those muscles dancing as he dragged the towel through his hair. So why did it feel so damned *right* watching him like this? *Wanting* him like this?

Then he froze.

Spun to fully face me.

And…I couldn't look away.

Not when the hand clutching the towel dropped to his side. Not when that brought my gaze back down.

To his penis.

Which garnered a good long stare, its length growing as it hardened under my watchful eyes. It swung slightly when he took a step toward me, his thighs flexing and drawing my gaze down toward those quads.

The black hair covering them did absolutely nothing to disguise their strength.

Especially as he strode toward me with complete casualness, seemingly not giving a damn that he was naked and gloriously erect when I managed to tear my eyes off his cock and bring them up to his face.

To the—no pun intended—cocky smile on his lips. To the molten heat that threatened to turn me to ash. To the—

He reached me, winding his fingers around my wrist and drawing me into the room.

All the air left my lungs, and only part of the reason was from my front colliding with his. The rest was...because my front had collided with his. Smitty was naked and strong, and his arms were wrapping around me, his masculine spice in my nose, the blazing heat of his body scorching through my clothes.

"Little bird," he murmured, his chin coming to the top of my head, his arms wrapped tight. "Oh, little bird, how am I going to punish you for spying on me?"

My breath caught. "Wh-what?"

A warm, broad hand smoothing over my hair, down my spine. "You're a peeping Tom," he murmured on a husky chuckle. "So, how should I punish you?"

My pulse picked up speed, battering its way through my veins.

Fingers on my chin, tilting my head up. "You like that," he murmured. "You like the idea of me punishing you."

A shaky inhale, my teeth finding my bottom lip, nibbling lightly.

His hand on my back dipped down, cupping my ass. "Should I smack this?" A rasping question paired with his cock pulsing against my stomach. "I'd give almost anything to see it turn red beneath my palm."

My knees wobbled, nearly giving way.

But he had me, that hand palming my ass keeping me flush against his naked body.

"You like that," he said again, eyes blazing into mine, head dipping down so our mouths were nearly aligned. "What else do you like, little bird?"

"I—" My words faltered when his tongue darted out, tasted my bottom lip.

"Yeah?" he pressed, verbally *and* physically, I realized distantly as he guided me farther into the room. "Sweetheart, what do you like a man to do to you?" he asked again, slowly hefting me up, a soft moan escaping me when my breasts rubbed against his chest.

My feet hit a bench, and though my legs were wobbly, he still held me tightly against him, one hand protecting the back of my head, making sure it didn't hit the shelves behind me. "I don't know."

My whisper had him freezing.

"Little bird," he said gently, his other hand cupping my cheek. "*Honey,*" he added when my gaze drifted to his shoulders (strong and broad and all too distracting).

I glanced back at him.

"Are you a virgin?"

Stiffness in my frame, a spinning in my stomach. Cheeks flaring. "No." I shook my head. "I've—"

I could shrink down.

Or...I could own it.

"I've slept with three men."

Careful eyes studying mine, as though judging my words for truth. Then the gentle faded and the mischief crept in. "So, I only have to kill three people," he teased. "That's doable."

"You're ridiculous."

He grinned. "Yeah, I am." His fingers trailed along my jaw. "And you're beautiful."

"I—" Another cheek flare, but he didn't seem to mind because his lips went there, pressing where my skin felt the hottest and then to the other side, tongue dipping out to taste the other heated spot. "You're the sexiest man I've ever seen."

Now it was his turn to blush.

And I got a firsthand view of how sexy it was.

This big man blushing over something *I'd* said? I wanted to recapture the moment, over and over again.

But later.

Because he was naked now.

And I was feeling like a heroine from one of my books. Sexy and powerful and strong. Confident and...turned on.

Right.

That was the biggest, most intense thing I was feeling. And it loosened my joints, my spine, had my body melting against his, my arms coming around his shoulders, feeling that bare, hot skin beneath my palms. "I don't know what I like," I murmured. "I've never even gotten close to having an orgasm with any of the men I've slept with." His head jerked, and I smoothed my hands down his chest. "But I read a lot." A breath and...I just went for it. "And I have a long list of fantasies."

Now his head jerk was joined by a wicked smile.

"Yeah?" he asked, pulling me tighter against him, bending his head so his lips trailed along my throat.

I nodded.

"Okay, little bird," he murmured against my skin.

Then he *moved*.

One second, I was standing on the bench, our bodies aligned, his mouth on my neck, and the next, he was flipping us so that he was sitting on the bench, and I was straddling his lap, and then he was kissing me.

Not gently.

Not tentatively.

But slamming his mouth onto mine, parting my lips, and tangling our tongues together. That big hand went back to my ass, the other dove into my hair, dislodging my ponytail, his low, deep rumble of a groan vibrating up through his chest, through mine, teasing my nipples, settling somewhere low inside me.

Okay.

It was in my pussy.

That deep, rumbling sound settled right in my pussy.

A nip to my mouth, his lips finding my jaw, sliding down, and sucking roughly at the spot where my shoulder met my throat. I suspected I'd have a mark there the next morning but couldn't bring myself to care.

Not when he'd yanked the hem of my shirt up and over my head, not when I was gasping as he buried his face in my breasts.

Not as one of his big hands was tugging my bra down.

My breasts popped free.

"Fuck me," he muttered. "I knew they'd be pink."

"Smitty," I whispered.

He glanced up at me, fire in his expression and need stark in the lines of his face. "Oh no, little bird," he said, clamping down on me when I began rocking on his lap, the hard length of his cock pressing against the seam of my leggings, causing the material to rub against just the right spot. "Not yet. You still haven't been punished."

I shivered. "Smitty," I whispered again, this time not bothering to hide the pleading in my tone.

A steady stream of warm air across my chest.

No. Across one nipple, then the other, the pink tips hardening, beading, begging for his mouth, his teeth and tongue. His hands. His chest.

Anything.

Just so he'd touch me.

Another stream. This one closer to the aching tip.

A flick of his tongue that had a moan tumbling from my tongue. A graze of his beard that had my hands going to his head, trying to pull him down.

He held firm. "No, little bird," he said, untwining my hands and placing them over my head, pressing lightly until I understood that he wanted me to grip the bottom of the shelf. "Don't let go," he ordered.

Then he leaned away, keeping me in his lap, but shifting so that his back was to the wall and my body was a few inches from his mouth.

He stared.

I quivered, hips jerking.

A hand clamping on my hip again, steadying me.

"Hold still and stay quiet, little bird," he murmured, and I did—holding my bottom half still against his pelvis, clamping my lips together.

"Good girl," he murmured before leaning in and repeating the treatment on my other breast.

Slowly, *interminably* slowly. A stream of air—gentle, then firmer, then closer.

Moving back and forth. Keeping up the blowing, giving me a little, the occasional flick of his tongue. But it wasn't enough. It wasn't everything. It wasn't what I *needed* with an almost clawing anguish that didn't relent. Not until I was absolutely trembling, sweat sheeting my body, gasps escaping, groans rising out of my throat.

A short, sharp suck that had me jumping.

"Quiet," he ordered, placing one finger to my mouth. "Or I won't do it again."

My chest rose and fell rapidly.

He bent, closed his teeth over one hard peak. "Yeah, little bird?" The words were so close to my skin that they felt like a physical caress, each syllable a damp touch that was sending me up a fragile edge. "*Little bird,*" he warned.

I nodded, shuddering again when one calloused fingertip ran over my beaded nipple. "Yes," I whispered. "I'll stay quiet."

The smile he gave me was pure fire.

And then, without the least bit of warning, he sucked my nipple deep.

My moan choked me, threatening to escape, but I bit my bottom lip hard, not wanting him to stop, desperate for him to keep going. And he rewarded me for the quiet—cupping my breasts and molding them, lifting one globe and then the other so he could suckle each of them in turn.

It was too much and not enough, and I was desperate...

For something.

For—

"Okay, little bird," he rasped against my skin. "Give me that mouth and *move.*"

His hand on my hip shifted, encouraging *me* to grind against him, and *that* was exactly what I needed. That pressure, that movement. The man beneath me and his hard cock. His mouth on mine, swallowing my moans. Still worshiping my breasts with one hand while the other arm banded around my waist, keeping me in motion, encouraging me to ride him faster and harder and—

That swelling of pressure began to coil tighter in my middle, the prerequisite to me flying over the edge.

One I'd never had outside of my own hands or my toys or—

Thoughts splintered when he tugged me slightly forward, changing the angle and—holy son of a dragon—*that* was incredible.

Actual sparks of light behind my eyelids and...

Implosion.

SEVENTEEN

Smitty

SHE'D COME for long enough that I seriously thought I was going to explode just from dry humping.

Like a fourteen-year-old boy.

But when I'd nearly reached the point of no return, she'd slowed, her movements going jerky, her forehead dropping to my shoulder, her hot breath on the bare skin of my chest.

"Holy shit," she whispered.

Yeah.

Seriously.

Her head shot up, nearly colliding with mine.

Luckily, I had quick reflexes and leaned out of the way, reaching up to slide her hands free of the shelf. Her skin was pale, as though the blood flow hadn't been good, and *no shit*, I thought. I'd had her clinging to the shelving with her arms above her head.

Slowly, I lowered her arms, massaging the skin gently,

getting the blood flow back and having the bonus of being able to touch her a little longer.

Eventually, though, she pulled back.

And I half expected her to pull back emotionally right along with physically.

Instead, though, she cupped my cheeks and kissed me deeply, breaking the kiss only after I felt like my lungs would explode.

She was breathing just as heavily when she straightened and smiled down at me. "Holy shit, Conner Smith, I should bronze you and perch you in the corner of my room as a statue of honor."

"Would you pray naked in my honor?"

Her smile widened. "Only if you asked really, *really* nicely."

I nuzzled her throat. "Oh, I'd ask nicely. I swear I would."

Mischief in green eyes. "Kind of like you *nicely* told me that you wouldn't let me come unless I shut up and held still."

"That's not—" Well, hell. I'd been playing, and I'd thought she'd been with me.

Fuck, what if she hadn't been?

What if I'd pushed her?

"I like to...um...play," I said quickly. "I thought you were...I mean...I thought you were with me." I held her stare. "Was it too much? Should I have—?"

Hands tilting my face up. "It was perfect," she said. "And the only orgasm that I've had..." Here she seemed to lose a little steam, her cheeks going pink. "The only one I've had with someone who wasn't me." She shrugged. "In case, it... um...wasn't clear earlier." Her hands lifted to her face, covering up all those gorgeous features. "I"—palms dropping, green eyes on mine—"could never come with them. Though—" She cleared her throat, gaze drifting away. "I didn't exactly do *this*"—a gesture between our bodies, during which she seemed to remember that she was topless, and her cheeks flushed again, her arms rising to cross over her breasts—"um, with *them.*"

I reached beside me, grabbing the towel that had somehow made its way to the bench and wrapping it around her shoulders, covering her breasts so that she wasn't so exposed.

Her fingers came to the edges of the white cotton, holding it closed. "How?" she whispered. "How do you always know?"

I shrugged. "I just...I look into your eyes, and I see you." My fingers trailed along her jaw, her skin like silk under my touch. "And I think part of it," I said, giving her the other piece that had been bouncing around my head since the morning a few days before, since she'd helped me with the personality test, "is that when I look at you, I see myself in a way."

Except, she was about a billion times smarter than me.

I was a brute, and she was brilliant. Beauty and the beast.

Big and loud and good at hitting shit. She was finesse and quietly competent.

We made no sense together—I knew that—but luckily for me, she seemed to feel the same connection that was pulling at me, drawing me like the opposite dipole of a magnet to her.

Her expression gentled. "I feel it, too," she whispered. "Like when you described what you've had to overcome, how you've had to learn to live with the dyslexia and how it sometimes seems to get worse when your emotions are high. I feel that. I mean, it's not the same. You have an actual clinical issue and mine is just...my mind getting away from me—"

Whoa.

"Kailey."

"My brain being weak and unable to cope—"

"*Kailey.*"

She stopped, stared up at me.

"What the fuck are you talking about?" I asked, and yeah, maybe my voice was a little too loud, a little too brusque.

Or not *too little* of either.

It *was* too loud and too brusque.

Because she jumped, shoulders slumping.

"Come here, little bird," I said, tugging her toward me, wrapping her tightly in my arms. "I'm sorry. I'm a big, loud oaf. But, honey," I went on, stroking my hand down her hair, "anxiety is a clinical diagnosis. It's real and it's a challenge, just like my dyslexia is for me."

"I know that," she said softly.

I pushed back her bangs. "But do you?"

A shaky breath. "I—" Her throat worked, even as her forehead fell forward and rested on my shoulder. "My family isn't exactly supportive of me in that way. They don't see it as a challenge, but rather, something to be ashamed of. And...they're impatient," she murmured. "And when I can't always step up and be Little Miss Charming—when I haven't *ever* been able to be that charming, carefree woman—their annoyance is like a palpable thing in the air, clawing at me from the outside while the ball of nerves shoots barbs at my insides, tearing me up."

Fuck.

I hated her family.

But I didn't want to add to that angst.

So, I just held her and kept stroking that hand down her hair, keeping her close and giving her the space to talk.

"They don't understand that I want to be normal, more than anything. I want to be able to walk into any situation and just be myself. I don't want it to take months for me to get comfortable, like it took with Oliver, like it took for me to even consider taking this job." Her head lifted. "Do you know why I only slept with three guys?"

"No, little bird," I said softly.

"It's because my first time I had a panic attack," she said, "and he didn't stop." Her lips pressed flat then curved up at the edges. "The only good thing was that he didn't take long."

My hand fisted in her hair, and I had to force myself to release it, to not yank at the delicate strands. One by one, I straightened my fingers, relaxed my palm, dropping it to her waist and clenching it into a fist there.

Still touching her, but the fury raging through me would mean that I wouldn't hurt her.

"The second time was in college," she whispered. "No panic attack, thankfully, but the whole thing didn't last much longer than the first time. A good thing," she added. "Because I think he watched that jackrabbit *Sex in the City* episode because I swear that my spine has never been the same."

A laugh.

I forced a smile.

Definitely two men I wanted to kill.

And that became three when she went on with the last time.

"It took me years to try again," she said. A shrug. "Until last year, actually," she added. "We went out a few times, and he was super patient when it came to me wanting to take my time. And...it was okay, but work had been tough around then and I'd had a bad day and after we were finished"—a shrug—"after *he* was finished, I just laid there, wondering if that was it." Her shoulders rose and fell again, this time on a sigh.

Three.

Definitely three men who deserved to die.

"What are their names?" I asked darkly.

She went still, fingers lightly trailing through my beard. "You want their social security numbers, too?"

"That would make the crimes I'd like to commit easier."

Gentle in her eyes, in her expression. "I'm a lot, Conner.

You need to know that." Her nails lightly ran along my jaw. "With you, it's easy," she said. "I don't understand completely why, but I'm going to take the gift the universe has given me."

The gift?

My heart squeezed. *Hard.*

"You're the gift," she said lightly. "In case you didn't get my not-so-subtle compliment."

"I'm not—" A shake of my head, not wanting to argue about that, not right then. "How are you *a lot?*" I asked.

"Besides the panic attacks?"

I nodded.

"I'm literally a ball of anxiety most of the time. I worry and rehash every single thing I say. I get nervous in social situations, and I can't form words—literally it's so fucking hard for me to say even one *fucking* word." A sigh. "I'm not good at sports. Hell, tonight was the first hockey game I'd watched, and Oliver spent the entire time explaining how the rules with that box thing worked—"

Rules?

I bit back a smile.

Her describing penalties as broken rules was adorable.

"I'm not competitive, so the whole plant competition is a fucking nightmare. And I push myself to interact with people, with others in the organization because they all seem really cool, but I mostly just avoid the invitations and escape to my place so I can read dirty books for masturbation material and take baths and—"

"Watch *Great British Bake-Off?*"

Her eyes narrowed. "Smitty," she warned.

My fists had relaxed, and I took a turn at cupping *her* cheeks. "What else?"

A frown. "Besides the anxiety that makes me mute and how I avoid situations when I should be forcing myself to be part of them because if I don't, I won't ever get better and how I don't know hockey and you're a hockey player—one who apparently had a fabulous game tonight that I couldn't even deduce because while I work for a professional team, I *don't know a thing about hockey?*" She tossed her hands up. "And the hyper analyzing of the things I *do* manage to say and the fact that my safe places are my bathtub and my computer?"

"Yeah, little bird," I murmured. "What else?"

"Did I mention the video games?"

Amusement flickered through me. "Yeah, honey, you did."

"And the baths and reading?"

A nod. "For the record, those are both pluses, especially when they send you flying like they did tonight or on the phone the other evening." I nipped the tip of her nose. "Bring on the dirty books and the woman who makes the sexiest sounds I've ever heard when she comes apart."

"And the hockey?"

"I don't give a fuck that you don't know hockey, little bird. It's been my life for as long as I can remember. I've lived and breathed and existed for the sport." I pushed back a strand of her hair, tucked it behind her ear. "I'm ready for something different."

I was, I realized.

I hadn't thought about it that way until the words slid off my tongue and hit the air.

But I was *so* fucking ready for Kailey.

"I've waited for you," I whispered. "For my whole life, I've waited for a woman like you."

Wide eyes, pink cheeks, parted lips. "I..." A breath, tears glistening in those wide eyes. "That is the most beautiful thing anyone has ever said to me," she whispered.

And I *had* to kiss her.

Had to taste the wonder on her face, the tears in her voice.

A racing heart, rightness settling onto my soul like a warm blanket, the first tendrils of love beginning to unfurl.

Then amusement when she pulled back, her lips swollen, and eyes slightly glazed.

"But did I mention the video games?"

CHAFING.

Definitely.

And paired with my sporting an erection for extended periods of time over the last week, one that had threatened to remove all the blood from my brain while casually shuffling it toward my dick, I'd decided that sweats were the way to go.

Along with a messenger bag.

Step one for comfort because I'd jerked off a pathetic number of times trying to get my dick to go down enough after Kailey had come apart on top of me.

Step two for disguising. Because the jerking off hadn't worked and I was still sporting an erection whenever I thought of her, or remembered the taste of her, or how her breasts had felt beneath my hands, the hard beads of her nipples on my tongue—

Fuck.

I shifted the bag as I walked into the rink, heading for Hazel's office.

Another meeting.

I was, apparently, the mental charity case this season, and not that I didn't think Hazel was cool, and I knew she was seeing other guys too and not just me, but...

It felt like she was looking too deeply.

I was supposed to be easy-come, easy-go, everything slides

off my back because I was the joker in the room and my job was to hit shit and make the guys laugh.

Simple.

This looking deeper shit wasn't good.

But Hazel had asked me to come, so I'd be there.

Because I could add reliable to my list of admirable qualities.

Because I'd do anything for the team.

EIGHTEEN

Kailey

I COULD BARELY LOOK at anyone the next day.

My only saving grace was that I was working at my office at the practice facility rather than the arena—and thus, nearby what would certainly be the forever blush-inducing locker room.

I still blushed a lot, though.

Mostly because the guys had the morning off with a light optional skate in the afternoon, so they'd begun occupying the player spaces, including the locker room at the practice rink, from fairly early in the morning.

Chatter had echoed through the hallways.

Big male bodies moving through at regular measure.

Something I'd seen because I'd kept my door open.

Hoping that a certain big male would poke his head in.

Last night, he'd gotten me dressed, and then himself, taking his time during the latter, and totally not caring that I'd done my share of staring at his unabashedly naked body, enjoying the way his muscles bunched and loosened, rippling under his skin, reminding me of the strength he'd used to hold me in place, the husky commands, all as he'd slowly pulled on his clothes.

The only time he looked mildly uncomfortable was trying to button up his slacks.

Which was mostly because he was making his own portable penis tent and trying to wrestle the monster in his pants down so he could tug up the zipper was no easy task.

I'd shocked the shit out of myself by offering to help.

And would never forget the shock on his face, and how that shock had transformed to glee when he'd realized I was playing with him.

Well, it was a serious offer because I did want to touch and stroke him.

But it was a serious offer for a later time, considering we were playing with fire already by having gotten half (me) and completely (him) naked in a public space. Where we both worked.

And...yeah.

Had I dreamed about him bending me over the bench, taking me from behind, driving me to another orgasm (since I knew he was fully capable of getting me there)? Yes.

Had I understood that we'd already taken enough risk? Unfortunately. Yes.

Plus, since I'd been thinking about risk—interspersed with all that naked ogling—I probably wouldn't have been able to concentrate on hanky-panky time.

Okay, probably not true.

I had the feeling that Smitty would be able to distract me. Anytime. Any day of the week. Any—

A knock on my open office door.

I head jerked, gaze flying up, anticipation coiling in my belly and—

Oh.

It wasn't him.

Two of the guys stood there...Raph and Theo. They'd been friendly and nice in my limited interactions with them so far, but that they were here? That anticipation coiling morphed into anxiety. It twisted and spun, sliding up to grip my lungs.

Theo nodded at the chairs in front of my desk. "Can we sit down?"

"Su—" My throat seized, but I managed to wave a hand to the pair of wooden chairs. They walked in, Raph all strong, bulky strength, mischief in his eyes, Theo leaner and with a ready smile. Folding into the seats, their big bodies taking up too much of the space in my office. Their gazes were on mine, making it hard for me to focus, impossible to speak.

But I could move, at least, so I grabbed a pencil and brought it to my lap, using it to keep my hands busy, to try to distract my mind from the spinning.

Take away the hyperfocus.

Redirect.

There wasn't impatience on their faces.

No, it was...eagerness. At least on Theo's. Raph's was placid, as though he were just there to watch things unfold—not in a cruel way, but rather like he was curious and wanted to see where things went.

Or at least, I hoped so.

Cruelty hadn't been something I'd experienced with this team.

I hoped that it continued not having a place here.

"Oliver said you play *Legends of the Dragons?*" Theo asked.

Okay, now *that* was a hard right in the conversation that I hadn't expected. Surprise had my throat loosening. Talk of something I was comfortable with even more so.

Or maybe it was that they didn't seem to be in any hurry.

Still, even though I'd gotten one syllable out.

Even though I was studying their faces, my heart pounding, searching for that impatience with half my brain, while the other half braced and also tried to formulate the proper response, vacillating between the two of them.

But even as they waited, as the silence stretched, nothing crept in. No snarky undertones or disappointment or barely concealed fury.

Just two men content to sit there until I got myself together.

The tension in my body relaxed, the pencil I'd been spinning in my hands slowing down until it stopped, and I managed to reach up and set it on my desk.

"Yes," I said. "I play it."

A ripple of excitement. "Please, tell me that you've gotten the new update. What do you think of...?"

He described some of the new types of game play—being able to look through their dragon's eyes as they flew, the new guild component and online cooperative quests, going on about them in a way that only a true fan of the game could. Which relaxed me further and I was able to chime in about my level and my guild name and the current quest.

"No way," he breathed. "I'm not nearly ready for that. My druid is only a level sixty-four."

I smiled. "I was lucky enough to work with one of the developers before he went off and started working on the game. He let me play a beta copy," I admitted. "So, I was able to get a jump on some of the inner workings when the real version was released."

His eyes went wide. "No *way*," he said again.

Which had me biting back a smile, because he wasn't all that young, maybe a year or two younger than my twenty-seven, but he was young in life, I thought. Sweet and kind and funny and...not saddled by a dark past.

Dark past?

My mother was more interested in her own life than mine, and my dad was an asshole.

A giant, insensitive asshole with a pocketful of money and an inferiority complex that meant he needed to make himself bigger and smarter and wealthier and *better* than everyone else.

Baggage, yeah.

But not exactly a dark past.

Or at least, I was trying to not live in the dark any longer.

A move, new friends—new *nerdy* friends I was actually able to talk to, even after Raph joined in on the conversation (though it was quickly evident that the widely-known prankster wasn't into video games and had tagged along for reasons only known to himself).

So maybe less of a dark past and more of a bright future.

Yeah, I liked the sound of that.

A lot.

"Did you want to see if I could get you an invite to my guild?" I offered unexpectedly, several minutes later.

Theo's face lit up. "You'd do that?"

I smiled. "Of course."

"That would be *epic*," he declared, showing me his youth again, and with his enthusiasm sweeping through the room, I felt very young, too. Young and light, or maybe bright and clean and...not anxious.

Myself.

I felt like myself.

First Oliver. Then Hazel and Smitty. Now Raph and Theo.

Next, I'd be raising my hand at meetings and demanding that I be able to talk.

Ha.

But it was a nice thought.

Today, I'd settle for an awkward conversation turning pleasant, for a new member of my guild and a few calmly exchanged words with Rafe. I'd take the goodbyes I managed to call out, and I'd take the bag Rafe asked me to pass on to Smitty.

No doubt the reason for the mischief on his face.

And the reason he'd tagged along.

"Why?" I asked as he handed over the bag. "Smitty and I—"

"He looks at you right, darlin'," Raph said lightly. "And"—he nodded at me—"you blush very prettily whenever his name is mentioned." He leaned in, asked quietly, "Want to tell me about it?"

"So, you can use it for blackmail?" I returned.

Then realized I'd made a mistake.

Because instead of denying anything was happening between me and Smitty—and I'd now been around the Breakers enough to understand that *not denying* was as good as confirming for the gossip-loving crew (sometimes everyone knew each other's business more than a small town in a romance novel)—I'd confirmed that something was already happening.

And it was blackmail worthy.

Shit.

That was...not good, very *not good.*

Raph surprised me by winking and tugging lightly at a strand of my hair. "Secret's safe with me."

Sure, it was.

But before I could say anything further or press him for details, he'd turned away, tossing a wave over his shoulder, and disappeared into the hall.

I glanced down at the bag, shook my head, and decided that I'd deal with it later.

NINETEEN

Smitty

I WALKED down the hall after my appointment with Hazel, glad that we didn't have any additional sessions scheduled.

I'd read through the papers she'd given me.

Was in agreement, for the most part, with what the results and additional information stated.

But that was as far as it went.

Interesting information.

What that had to do with improving the team, I didn't know.

Of course, I couldn't say *that*. Hazel was good at her job, and probably had her reasons, so I was just going to go along with what she said, strap in and take that roller-coaster ride, and leave the majority of my focus for the team.

And for Kailey.

Because *that* was more interesting than understanding why my brain worked the way it did.

Now, I'd finished with Hazel, needed to get ready for practice.

But...I needed to see Kailey.

So, I was bypassing the locker room, slipping down the hall as sneakily as my big ass frame could, and determined to sneak a few moments with the woman who was responsible for all my...chafing.

my lips were curved as I peeked into the office.

Then curved further when I regarded the scene in front of me.

Her hair piled on top of her head, a pair of tortoiseshell glasses perched on her nose. She was curled up in her chair, gaze on her computer, fingers moving rapidly across the keyboard.

Beautiful.

Sexy as fuck.

My office fucking fantasy I hadn't known I possessed flaring to the forefront of my mind.

And then she looked up, saw me standing there...and her face softened, the corners of her mouth turning up into a small smile. "Hi," she said shyly, pink appearing on her cheeks.

"Little bird," I murmured.

Her hand lifted, pushed a strand of hair off her face, tucking it behind her ear.

"I dreamed of you last night."

She shivered.

I crossed to her. "Cold?" I asked, leaning a hip against her desk, close to where her right arm rested.

That arm rose, brushing my thigh, making my cock twitch, and dropped onto her lap. "You know very well that I'm not cold," she said, and fuck, I loved when she got a little pert with me. I wanted to hear that same tone ordering me around in bed.

My stare flicked to her chest, to where the hardened buds

of her nipples were pressing against her shirt. "I don't know"—I shifted a little closer—"you seem a little cold to me."

Those cheeks went pinker, but her chin lifted an inch, and her eyes narrowed.

"God, you're sexy with those glasses and your hair like that," I said. "Will you play teacher-student with me? Or librarian and naughty patron who's making too much noise in the reference section?"

Her mouth dropped open. "*Smitty,*" she exclaimed.

"What?" I asked innocently, then shifted the messenger bag so it was covering my crotch...and my twitching dick that would soon be a full-fledged erection if I didn't stop thinking about naughty librarians...

Or patrons.

Or Kailey as a teacher, pulling out her ruler and—

Focus.

I managed to, but Kailey was already turning away from me, reaching down by her feet. "I didn't want to do this," she said softly, her breasts bouncing lightly as she straightened, "but the guys picked up on what happened between us, and"—her eyes flicked to the bag she'd retrieved from the floor—"after *that*"—a gesture toward my body, face to hips—"I have no choice."

Okay, so my and Kailey's relationship already being picked up by the Breakers gossip fiends wasn't ideal.

I'd been hoping to keep her to myself for just a little while longer, to avoid the nosey fuckers and the gossip and what would no doubt be deemed *"helpful"* interference.

At least for a few days.

Because I wasn't exactly slick.

My feelings were big and loud and, hell, even that personality test I'd taken said I wasn't good at hiding what was in my heart.

What people saw, they got with me.

She pushed back, sliding the black cloth-covered chair away from me, and I went from disappointed at her moving away from me to distracted from the thoughts of the gossip and my heart on my sleeve to distracted by her body again when I saw her curves filling out her jeans.

Now, if she'd only turn around.

Because, fuck, I liked that ass.

Her breasts were everything I'd imagined they'd be.

But, God, I wanted her ass naked and my hands on it, squeezing the twin globes, dragging my mouth over it, my teeth, my tongue.

And miracle of fucking miracles, she turned enough to give me a glimpse of her ass in those jeans as she started to push her chair back into her desk.

"You don't have any comment on that?" she asked archly, her eyes hitting mine over her shoulder and fuck, this little tart, this gorgeous, beautiful sexual woman, was driving me absolutely crazy.

She moved to stand in front of me.

One more kiss.

One more taste.

I wanted...*more.*

Fucking hell, I *wanted* more.

"Oh?" I countered, not remembering in the least what the fuck we were talking about, only holding my breath as she shifted a little closer, her thighs brushing mine. She lifted an arm, rested it on my arm.

Except, that brought the material of her shirt tight over her chest.

Over her breasts.

Oh, I wanted my mouth back on those, too.

Her hand slid down my arm, opening my palm, pulling my

fingers flat, but I was too fucking focused on her breasts to notice what she was putting in my hand, especially when the movement of her arm made those fucking perfect tits bounce and—

"Open it."

I blinked, looked down between our bodies, and saw the medium-sized gift bag hanging off one hand.

Obediently, I pulled out the tissue paper, reached in.

"They said I should give it to you because you like—"

I pulled out the item...and squealed.

Yes, like a little bitch.

And then, yeah, it was a pussy move, but I launched the furry stuffed toy away from me, shuddering. "What the fuck?" I exclaimed, eyes hitting hers. "What the *actual* fuck?"

She frowned, uncertainty hitting her expression for the first time in a while with me, and I hated that I'd put it there.

But that...

That, *sir*, was a fucking wombat and...

Jesus Christ.

I shuddered again, cradled her against my chest as I kicked it farther away from me with the very toe of my boot.

She pulled out of my hold, crouched, flashing me that ass, and it was almost enough for me to move toward her, to go near that thing, and take her in my arms and—

"Don't," I began.

She rose, holding the stuffed toy in her hands.

And I had to physically ground myself to not move back. Fuck. The thing had little black beady eyes that were piercing straight into my soul.

"Do you not—?" Her eyes flicked to mine then down to the monster she held. "Are you *scared* of a...wombat?"

"Don't say their name," I said, averting my gaze, and in doing so, seeing that we'd gained an audience.

Theo and Raph were in the doorway, arms crossed, mouths turned up into a smirk.

Were they fucking serious right now?

They were trying to usurp my role as the ultimate shit-giver, prankster, and they were doing it in front of *Kailey*? Getting her involved. *My* woman involved.

"You fuckers," I growled, taking a step toward them.

Their smirks increased in wattage.

"Conner."

Her soft voice drew my gaze back to hers.

She still held the toy.

"Can you—?" A nod that had her glancing down at her hands, biting back a smile. But she set the toy down on her desk, and I ignored her eyes dancing with mirth.

Then she stepped closer. "I didn't know," she whispered. "No, that's not fair. I knew Raph was up to some mischief." She pressed her palm to my cheek then bit and released her bottom lip. "But I didn't think it was something that would scare you. I'm sorry."

I liked when there was fire in her eyes.

I hated the uncertainty that had drifted in during this conversation.

So, I ignored the fuckers in the hallway. I'd deal with them later. Then I moved to her, took her tiny, capable hands in my own, and brought her close.

Progress that she didn't resist me, even in front of our audience, when she let me pull her close. "They're just fucking with me. Don't worry about it."

Concern in those green eyes. "Why?"

My mouth turned up. "Because we're hockey players and around each other too much and we're basically overgrown children and—" I shrugged. "It's what we do. What *I* do. Keeps the room light. Just usually..."

Her face went gentle, but a bit of laughter danced along the edges. "It's you who gives the shit, instead of receiving it?"

"I—"

"He means yes," Raph chimed in.

Unhelpfully.

That was an *unhelpful* chime in. For the record.

In case anyone was wondering.

"Why are you fuckers still here?" I growled over my shoulder.

Now *delight* danced in her eyes. "Is this part of being friends?" she teased. "Are you going to give me shit?"

Now delight danced in my *stomach*, bubbling up and sliding through my veins, filling me with happiness. "I'm gonna give you *something*," I muttered.

She grinned. "God, I hope so."

A wave of heat. My cock dangerously close to needing that shield again. "What is it for you?" I asked. "Not wombats, obviously. Spiders? Snakes? The creepy crawlies that live on our skin?"

Her head tilted to the side, studying me. "Why would I tell you that?" she asked softly.

"Because that's what friends do?"

"Is that what we are?" Her teeth pressed into her bottom lip, but this time it appeared that she was attempting to conceal a smile. "Because I kind of thought what happened yesterday meant..."

"What happened yesterday?" Raph asked, the fucker drawing me out of the conversation, and I knew those fuckers were still in the doorway, probably able to hear every word and preparing to give me shit for it and—

"Hold that thought," I said softly, stroking the backs of my knuckles along her throat, dipping into the slight v of her top. Then I stepped back and moved to the door, shoving the guys out. "Fuck you," I said, glaring at Theo. "And fuck *you*," I snapped at Raph.

Then the door was slammed.

I spun back...

The wombat had made itself a home on top of her monitor.

TWENTY

Kailey

"EVIL," he murmured, prowling toward me.

Yeah *prowling*.

I shivered, but it was only in anticipation. There wasn't any fear, any anxiety, no ball of nerves in my belly spreading outward, slicing as it expanded. Just heat prickling between my thighs, my nipples tingling as they remembered the treatment he'd given them the night before, my palms itching to touch, my pussy clenching and empty and...a little desperate.

But I was feeling...ballsy.

So damned ballsy.

And I wanted to tease, to give him back some of that teasing.

I lifted my hand, stroking it along the soft fur of the stuffed toy. "I've decided to name him, Herman."

His beard twitched. "Herman?"

Right. Not the best name, but the only one I'd thought of on the spot. I might be finding a bit of myself, clawing out from beneath the tangled web of my insides, but I still wasn't the best improviser.

Probably wouldn't ever be.

But being comfortable with Smitty meant that I could lift my chin, could smile sweetly, and pat the stuffed wombat on its adorable little head. "Yes, *Herman* is his name, and he's so cute that he's going to be living here in my office."

That beard twitched again, but I noticed that his gaze didn't stray to Herman again, just stayed locked onto mine.

He stepped closer.

And...my heart started to beat a little faster.

Thud-thud. Thud-thud. Thud-thud.

A twining, writhing net, but not one that sent me spiraling into anxiety or fogging my brain—or at least, not one that fogged my brain in a way that wasn't cramming me full of need and nearly sending me begging for him to press his mouth to mine again, to touch my breasts, to strip me naked and worship the rest of me.

No fear.

No worry of the words that may or may not cross my tongue.

Just...desire.

"You gonna climb me like a tree again, little bird?" he murmured, his voice rasping over me and raising goose bumps on my skin. "Or hold silent and still again while I take care of you?"

My pulse was fluttering...much like a little bird. Because I did want to climb him like that tree, wanted to cling to the branches of his arms and to feel the rustle of his breath on my skin. I wanted to hold still, and I wanted to *move.*

I wanted it all.

I was learning about myself.

And him.

And myself *with* him.

He liked to tease and joke and banter. I wanted to be the type of person who could do that with him. I wanted to be the type of person who could do that in *general*.

So...practice.

With a six-foot-plus hockey player and a stuffed wombat.

Oh, my life was *so* hard.

Woe was me.

"No," I said, "I think I've held still enough." I smiled slyly. "Maybe I'll make *you* hold still." A grin now. "Blindfold you and pretend that Herman is a feather or—*ah!*" My teasing ended with a squeak, and I couldn't even be embarrassed because Smitty had me up in his arms, my legs automatically going around his waist, my back pressed to the wall, and his front...oh good gravy, his front was pressed to mine.

I *loved* when we held each other like this.

Strong shoulders. Big pecs. Hard...stomach.

Another grin, but then I was wrapped up in the *strength* of him and it made me feel warm and secure and...very *very* turned on.

His breath puffed on my skin, raising goose bumps on my arms, my nape, my back.

"This going to become a thing?" he asked huskily.

My chin lifted, eyes hitting his, studying the deep brown of his irises, the dark russet and lighter oak weaving together to form something that was absolutely breathtaking.

"What? Me and you naked with Herman joining the fun?" I asked innocently.

He bent, nipped my bottom lip, and I was still processing the flash of movement, the bristle of his beard, the slight bite of pain when his mouth came down harder on mine, when he parted my mouth and slipped his tongue inside, dancing it along mine in a way that had my fingers diving into his hair, drawing him closer, tangling my tongue with his.

He kissed like fire.

And I was so beyond happy to embrace the flames.

Hell, I loved the feel of them licking down my spine, sinking into my arms, my legs, my pelvis. Burning through me, turning me to ash, reforming me into something magical and fresh and...comfortable in myself.

It was a gift.

It was the *best* gift that this man had given me.

He released my lips, and I sighed in pleasure, sucking in a breath when his mouth trailed along my jaw, nipping and kissing before dragging lower, tongue dipping down and in to trace along my collarbone.

"Okay, if it's not Herman, what thing are you referring to?" I asked, still going for innocent, though my voice had gone husky. "Quality time in the locker room? Brainstorming in my office?"

His head shot up, eyes blazing. "Oh, the kissing you thing is definitely going to be a *thing*." A beat. A kiss to my nose. "And the locker room thing, too, hopefully." Another kiss to my jaw. "Definitely the brainstorming thing in your office. *That's* going to be a thing—a fucking awesome *thing*."

"That's a lot of *things*," I breathed.

He grinned, and I could feel the same stupid grin on my face.

Okay, his wasn't stupid, just a bit dopey. Much like how my own felt, and *okay*, that wasn't the point, but I had a lot of *points* floating around in my brain, not the least of which was me thinking that I really just wanted him to kiss me again because he was fucking good at it.

Oh, and also, I was closer to an orgasm from one of Smitty's kisses, from him holding me, than I'd ever been with any of the men who'd been *inside* me.

Oh...and he also felt really great pressed up against me.

Oh...and...I was seriously considering desk sex.

We'd already done the locker room thing, maybe it was time for—

He shifted, pressing into me a little harder, making my breath catch and a wave of need wobble through me. "But we're going to do a lot of other *things*, too."

"I thought we were just going to be friends."

His hands—one cupping my ass, one threaded through my hair—tightened. "Oh, little bird," he said with a smirk. "We're going to be friends. Really *good* friends." The hand on my ass slid down. In. "*Best* friends who do *lots* and *lots* of *things* together."

"Yeah?" I countered.

His head dipped, mouth coming closer, and my lips parted immediately. "Yeah?"

I couldn't resist asking, "Do friends kiss?"

"*My* best friend and I do," he murmured huskily.

"Oh, I didn't know that you and Raph kissed," I said, going for breezy. "That's hot."

His lids, which had slowly been sinking closed—presumably giving in to the same desire that was relentlessly drawing me down—flew open, and those deep brown eyes locked onto mine, humor flickering across the depths. "You're sassy, little bird."

My head tilted to the side. "Not normally."

A grin.

"You're sassy with *me*." He seemed proud of that fact.

I bit my lip. "Yeah," I agreed.

His mouth curved, that beard twitching. "Fuck," he said,

confirming my thoughts. "I really love that you're sassy with me, little bird."

"You don't want me quiet and compliant?" It was said jokingly, but my relationship with my dad meant that a small part of me *did* wonder if men wanted that.

"God, no." He shuddered. "Give me the sass and the fire. Give me *everything*, little bird."

"You keep calling me that," I murmured. "Why?"

"Why *little bird*?"

A nod.

"That's for me to know and not you."

My lips pressed flat. "What if I peck your eyes out?" I asked tartly. "Would you like it then?"

His mouth turned up, just at the edges. "Depends."

"On what?" I asked, genuinely curious.

"On whether or not you're touching my dick when you do that."

Laughter bubbled up in my throat, burst forth, his husky chuckles joining in and drifting over me like the softest velvet.

Then he kissed me again.

Kissed me until there was a loud knock at the door, until Raph's voice echoed through the panel, calling out that Smitty better move his ass or else he was going to be late to practice.

A sigh as he released me, slowly allowing my feet to hit the floor.

He crouched slightly. "Dinner tonight?"

I sucked in a breath, suddenly felt perched on a precipice, unsure of which side to topple.

But that only lasted a moment.

Because I knew *exactly* which side I wanted to fall.

TWENTY-ONE

Smitty

THE PUCK FLEW through the air, coming straight for my face.

I swiped a hand up, used my glove to bat it down.

Cas, who was lining up to my right, smirked, "Just making sure that moony expression you're wearing hasn't affected your reflexes."

"Dude," I muttered, flicking the puck over to my line mate. "Not you, too."

"Of course, me too, man." Cas caught the pass, swiped it back to me. "You're the biggest shit-giver in the room. This is the greatest thing that's ever happened to me, being able to give you crap about being *smitten* with Kailey."

Anger prickled through me. "Why wouldn't I be smitten over her, assholes? She's fucking—"

"She's great," Cas interrupted. "I'm just loving that you're whipped after giving Marcel and Oliver and Luc so much shit about it."

Except, I might have given my friends shit, but Pru knew that I'd been longing for someone who saw me for who I was and didn't find me lacking or dysfunctional. She'd given me the advice that had allowed me to recognize what I was feeling with Kailey, to not be scared of going for it.

Because I saw my friends being happy.

Because I wanted that, too.

Because...I was willing to put my heart on the line to find what they had.

So, I might give them shit, but we all knew that I was really fucking jealous—or *had* been jealous.

Kailey was...

Enough to take my breath away.

And even though we were new, even though I'd just gotten her to begin trusting me, I knew this was *everything*.

I still didn't like being on the receiving end of the shit-giving, though I could admit that I deserved it.

"Well, you suck at giving shit, so you should just give up," I grumbled, whipping the puck back over.

"Well, *you* suck...at..." His eyes flicked to the side. "Insert a lot of things I can't think of right now because Jake is giving me that look that says we'd better stop fucking around otherwise he's going to dump a boatload of new drills on us, and I really don't feel like dying on the ice this afternoon." He grinned. "I met this girl last night"—he brought his glove to his mouth, a la a chef's kiss—"and she invited me over tonight for homemade pasta." Another chef's kiss. "Hockey. Carb loading. Fucking. The perfect trifecta of the day."

I couldn't disagree with that.

I also didn't want to be on the receiving end of any extra drills from Jake.

So, I resisted the urge to punch my D partner in the throat, dealt with the quiet, albeit, not so subtle shit-giving that was tossed my way, from Cas and pretty much everyone else—though I made a mental note to start plotting—

A mental note that grew into a mental billboard after I walked into the locker room and found my stall stuffed full of creepy as fuck plush wombats.

Why?

Why the beady eyes?

Why, God?

Grabbing a stick, I knocked them away from my space—ignoring the fucking cackles from the guys and *definitely* plotting some serious revenge.

***

"I FEEL like you should lead with the Stanford alum part," I said lightly, reaching over and topping off her glass with beer.

I'd wanted to take her someplace nicer than CeCe's—the bar me and most of the Breakers organization hung out at on the regular—but Kailey had asked to come here, saying she'd heard everyone talk about it and would like to see the place for herself.

Also, it was really early for dinner.

None of the nice places were open yet.

So, we were sitting on barstools at a high-top table, my feet on the bottom rung, Kailey's swinging lightly as she sat next to me. A basket of mozzarella sticks was in front of us. A plate of nachos next to that. Both had been pretty much decimated, but the salad I'd ordered—wanting to pretend to be at least a little bit healthy—was untouched.

Now we were working our way through a pitcher of beer, sitting around, chatting about our pasts.

She'd been a little jumpy at first and had stammered her

way through ordering, glancing at me a half-dozen times, like she'd expected me to explode in frustration.

I hadn't, of course.

When I'd been in all my interventions in school, trying to figure out how to read initially, and then, later, the techniques to make it easier, I'd *hated* when I'd felt the impatience of the person helping me. Sometimes it was verbal—a sharp "come on" or "hurry up." But the majority of the time it was nonverbal —a shifting, a sigh, a head bob, or a hand flicking.

I'd gotten really good at picking up on all of those things, tuning into that impatience, trying absolutely anything to stop it from coming to a head.

Kailey was that way, too.

Maybe that was why my soul felt comfortable with hers.

And the longer I'd waited, the more patient I'd been, the more she'd relaxed. The easier it had been for her to be there, in a new place with people all around—or at least, from what I'd presumed.

Her face had relaxed.

She hadn't gotten that wide-eyed, panicked look I'd seen at the barbecue—which had brought me to a slight side tangent of hating myself for how I'd handled that initial interaction, not recognizing the signs, wishing I had and—

"What?" she asked softly, her hand finding my arm.

"I'm just thinking about the barbecue."

She shuddered. "Oh *that*," she whispered. "Not my idea of a good time." She released my arm, picked up the last mozzarella stick, offered it to me, and when I shook my head, took a big bite, washing it down with a sip of her beer. "But," she said, when she'd swallowed, "I'm getting better at it."

"I think you're doing incredible."

"You should have seen me before," she whispered, a little shyly. "And you'd really think that." Her fingers wrapped around my forearm again, and I fucking loved that she was seemingly touching me without thinking, comfortable enough that her body found mine.

Like Lexi to Luc.

Like Hazel to Oliver.

Like Pru to Marcel.

I was part of that solar system now, a pair of planets orbiting each other, or maybe I was the moon to Kailey's—

"It's easy with you all," she said softly. "I don't know if it's the fresh start, or you all are just really nice, but"—she took a breath—"it feels like my lungs work better here."

"All that sea air," I said lightly.

A grin. "Maybe."

Fingers through her hair, the shorter pieces that framed her face falling forward to tease her cheeks. "Or maybe it's that we're all nice."

She snorted now, humor dancing across her face. "No, baby," she murmured. "You're not nice. *Very* not nice."

My hand found its way to her thigh, fingers splaying, feeling the heat of her pussy blazing even through the denim of her jeans. Her color went high, leg twitching. I slid it up an inch. Two. "Should we see how very *not* nice I can be, little bird?"

"Why?"

My brows furrowed. "Why what?"

"Why do you call me that?"

The hard left in our conversation threw me for a minute, but then I caught the hint of naughtiness in her expression, her lips fighting a smile.

And I couldn't resist bending my head, slanting my mouth over hers, and kissing the shit out of her.

Right in the bar.

Where anyone might see.

Where...she might be uncomfortable.

Fuck.

I pulled back, slowly, because it was almost impossible to have my lips on hers, my tongue in her mouth, and then just *stop* kissing her.

But I managed to straighten away from her, *though* I did pull her stool even closer so that I could turn and put my legs on the bottom rung of the stool on either side of her, trapping my little bird in place.

She leaned back against my chest, eyes glazed and lips damp and swollen.

And the need to kiss her again was nearly overwhelming.

A hand on my cheek.

Her thumb tracing over my lips.

"Why'd you stop?" she asked.

Fuck, why *had* I?

Because she was staring up at me, need written into the lines of her face, her body pressed to mine, and I was trying, searching desperately for a reason to not take her into the hall and find a storage room, a bathroom, hell a semi-dark fucking alley to alleviate this need that was burning through me.

Kailey first.

Kailey first.

I sucked in a breath, wincing when it bounced her against my chest. Placing a palm between her shoulder blades, I steadied her. "I thought you might be uncomfortable with the PDA."

A quiet chuckle, her head tilting back so that her chin rested on my sternum.

And fuck, what I wouldn't give to have her naked and on top of me and staring at me like that.

Then she totally undid me by saying, "Smitty, baby, do you think I could ever be anything but comfortable with you?"

I went still, those words tearing through me, burning and breaking, reducing me to pieces and ash, and then I was whole again. Only this time, it was more. *I* was more.

Because of her.

Holding her against me, I dug out my wallet, threw some bills on the table, and signaled to Julie, our server, that we were out of there.

Then she was on her feet, eyes going wide, body leaning into me as I steadied her.

"What's the matter?"

I bent, nipped her earlobe. "What's the matter?" I asked, flicking out my tongue, tasting her, hearing the moan that escaped her lips. "*What's* the matter?"

A shudder. "Y-yes," she whispered. "What's—?"

I grabbed her hand, tugging her out of the room, narrowing my eyes at Julie when she smirked. She just waved and mouthed, "Another one bites the dust."

And I couldn't be annoyed with her for the teasing.

I was completely gone for Kailey.

Especially when she told me things that were a big deal. A *really* big deal.

I pushed through the outside door, still towing her along, but the cool air seemed to spark her to action, and she began dragging her heels. "Smitty," she said, tugging at my hold. "No. *Stop.* Tell me what's the matter, baby."

Baby.

Fuck.

I turned, thanking God we'd parked out back.

Because one second, I was intent on getting her to my car, and the next I was on her.

Lifting her into my arms, encouraging (though she was pretty much doing it automatically by now) her legs around my waist. I pressed her into the wall, barely remembering to slide a hand behind her head so that it was protected.

Her hands came to my face. "Your eyes," she whispered. "What is it?"

And I wondered how much of the crazed feeling that was twisting through me showed on my face.

Because what she'd said. The endearments.

Ash again.

To be put in a little jar solely for her possession.

"You," I said.

She blinked.

"You're fucking wonderful."

She blinked again.

Then a slow smile built on her face, as though I were watching her erect it brick by brick. Small then larger. Gentle then wicked.

Wicked.

Because her palm was snaking down between us, drifting for the waistband of the sweats I hadn't bothered to change because we'd just been going to CeCe's.

But now there was no shield.

No barrier.

And her fingers slid beneath.

I caught her hand, brought it to my mouth.

She shivered when I pressed a kiss to her palm, but then she slid that palm down, her arm coming around my shoulders as she leaned in.

"You're fucking wonderful, too."

My dick got even harder. My hand on her hip clenched, trying to resist the urge to thrust into her. "*This*, little bird. *This* is what's the matter. I'm two seconds away from fucking you in broad daylight in a parking lot."

Still.

A tiny, gorgeous statue in my arms.

Then...she giggled. Her other hand coming up and wrapping around the side of my neck, her laughing eyes meeting mine. "I'm comfortable with you, baby. But maybe not quite ready for public fucking."

I groaned, dropped my head to her shoulder.

"Killing me, little bird. Killing me."

"I'll stop if you tell me why you call me that."

Laughter bubbled in my chest, and I held her closer. "Now," I murmured, nipping at the side of her throat, "how am I going to punish you for *that* bit of snark?"

TWENTY-TWO

Kailey

"OH FUCK," I whispered. "Oh *fuck.*"

Smitty had driven me to my place, promising to pick me up in the morning since my car was still at the rink.

He'd come in.

I hadn't explicitly invited him to, but I also hadn't thought I *had* to. Because there wasn't any doubt that our night wasn't over.

The sun was still up.

I wasn't remotely tired.

I didn't want him to go.

Thankfully, he seemed content to stay as well.

He'd followed me into the kitchen, and I'd offered him another beer as I'd given him the tour of my place—which took all of two minutes, since it was a tiny apartment. The Breakers paid well, I had a huge trust fund (one that I didn't touch, because my father already had enough strings in my life that he liked to pull and manipulate), and my extra income from side projects. I could afford a bigger place, but it was just me. I didn't need a ton of space.

The small apartment was a benefit that evening.

Because my bed was in the same room as my TV, and after we'd made the rounds, I'd asked if he'd wanted to watch a movie.

We'd started on the couch, eating out of a bag of popcorn I'd popped in the microwave.

But we hadn't watched the movie.

Instead, about ten minutes into the car chase kicking off the action flick, Smitty had snagged the remote, turned on a certain British reality TV baking show, and he'd turned hot eyes on mine.

I'd reached him first, launching myself into his arms, plunking down onto his lap.

And now...

He'd carried me to bed at some point, I'd lost my top again, he'd lost his, and—

"Oh fuck," I breathed, back arching, his hands all over me, his mouth finding my nipples, his hand reaching down between us and flicking open my jeans.

Yes.

I wanted that.

But also, he'd done all the touching so far.

I wanted to get my hands, my mouth on him.

So, I snagged his hand, drew it back up to my breast, and rolled into him. He was so big that I wouldn't have been able to move him like that if he hadn't let me, and the heated grin he sent my way when I ended up on top of him, told me why.

"Fuck, I love these," he muttered, reaching for my breasts again, massaging them, rubbing his thumbs over my nipples, sending liquid desire between my legs, shivers dancing along my spine, need coiling in my belly.

"I love *this*," I murmured, stroking my hands down his chest. Big muscles, a light covering of hair, flat abs, and biceps that bulged as he worked my breasts.

Distracting me.

But I was on a mission.

And that mission was getting to touch the monster in his pants.

A stroke of his thumb along either side of my mouth. "Why you smiling, little bird?"

"I'm excited"—I shifted, tugged the waistband of his sweats—"that I finally get to feel this."

Now *he* was smiling. "You've *already* felt it."

Heat washing over me. My pussy convulsing, feeling all too empty. But I was a woman on a mission, and *that* mission was getting my hands and mouth on his cock.

His cock sprang free.

And yeah, it was even more gorgeous up close.

Standing hard and stiff and thick, veins pulsing along the sides, a bead of moisture on the tip. "Well," I murmured, dragging the flat of my tongue along his shaft, "I want to feel *more* of it." And then I sucked him into my mouth.

I hadn't done much of this, felt like I was fumbling, especially when I couldn't get much of him in without feeling like I was choking.

But he didn't seem to care.

"Fuck, little bird," he murmured, hips flexing, hands coming to my head, fingers weaving into the strands of my hair. He didn't push down, was just touching me, staying connected to me. "Yes, oh my God, Kailey. That's really fucking good. Yeah, your tongue, flick your"—his hands flexed—"*fuck*, right there, honey. Right—"

He pulled me off, flipped me over, moving me like I weighed nothing.

Then his mouth was on mine, his tongue moving deep, his hands tracing up and down my sides, teasing my breasts before heading down, opening my jeans again.

Under my panties.

A warm hand on my pussy.

Finding my clit without a searchlight, pressing it hard, rocking it back and further.

"Oh fuck," I breathed.

But some part of me didn't want to find this alone. I wanted this with him. So, I managed to reach between us, to grip his cock and start stroking it in a rhythm that matched what he was doing between my legs.

"Little bird," he said roughly, "you don't have to—"

I leaned up enough to press a kiss to his mouth. "Don't stop," I ordered, stroking faster. "Don't stop and I won't."

Hot brown eyes on mine.

My chin lifted, and I met the challenge in them.

Then he smiled. "Fuck, little bird, I can't wait to punish you for this later."

I couldn't either.

But, for the moment, I kept stroking, and he continued rubbing my clit, slipping a finger home, stretching me with that big, thick finger.

It wasn't enough, not nearly.

But it was enough for that moment.

Because he was working me, and I was close, gloriously close. Thankfully, I knew that he was right there with me, his body beginning to tremble, his hips jerking, those fingers on me moving faster, harder.

Exactly what I needed.

"Smitty," I moaned.

"Fuck, little bird, your hand is fucking magic." His cock

grew, hardened further. "If you don't stop, I'm going to come," he warned. "I'm—"

He pressed my clit hard with the pad of his thumb.

I was the one who came apart.

But he wasn't far behind me, his body shaking, his hand by my head clenching into the blankets, his hips jerking.

And then, as the waves of pleasure began to subside, I felt it.

Hot jets of cum landing on my chest, dripping over my hand. His head dropped forward, he pushed into my grip, and his groans mingled with mine.

Fuck.

That was hot.

He collapsed to the side, not caring that I was a mess, tucking me against him, his chest rising and falling rapidly. I was no better, feeling like I'd run...well, not a marathon, because that wasn't my thing, would never be my thing. But definitely a 5K.

Eventually, our breathing slowed, and he got up, striding into the bathroom and returning with a damp cloth.

It was warm, I realized as he wiped me clean.

He'd waited for the water to get warm before cleaning me up.

A little piece of my heart broke off, sailed right through space, and landed in his lap.

And when he got up, took care of the towel, and came back, tugging the blankets up and over me, I knew that he'd keep it safe.

THE FOLLOWING WEEK, I pushed into my office, feeling a little down that Smitty was going to be away for the next eight days on an extended road trip.

It was part of the system, and since I wasn't an essential member of staff, I wouldn't be traveling with the team.

Normally, that would have thrilled me.

Not having to people?

But it wasn't people when it was this team, these people who were becoming mine.

Hazel was staying—because she didn't travel with the team either—but Pru was flying out, using the first part of the trip as a jumping point for her job as a scout. She'd be home before the guys, though, since her scouting wasn't going to take as long.

How did I know all this?

The day before, as I'd been getting ready to leave and go to my place for dinner and another make-out-slash-oral-sex-extravaganza evening that ended with me falling asleep in Smitty's arms, and him tucking me into bed before leaving in the wee house of the morning to catch his flight, Hazel had come into my office and asked me to go out to dinner with her in a couple of days on Thursday night with her friend, Beth, along with Pru, and Raph's pregnant girlfriend—new fiancé—Monica.

Thursday night apparently meant it was Cheese Extravaganza Night.

Which sounded incredible (although not as incredible as the Oral Sex and Touching His Yummy Body Extravaganzas I'd had with Smitty), especially since it was at CeCe's, and I not only had a special place in my heart for the restaurant and bar because it was where I and Smitty had gone that first night, but also because...cheese.

Yum.

More than that, I'd said *yes*.

I'd said yes.

Without nerves coiling in my stomach, without my throat closing up and words stoppering up in the back of it, without worrying—too much, anyway—that there would be new people there I hadn't met before.

Not Beth, who was lively and energetic and impossible not to like. I had met her a few times since she'd begun working for the team, as she, Pru, and Hazel were all very close and she visited often now that her two best friends lived in Baltimore.

But Monica was an unknown element.

Still, I'd been crushing the anxiety game of late.

It was time to keep working on it.

And if Monica was a troll, at least I would get fried cheese.

Win-win.

Smiling as I closed my office door, I flicked on the lights and...stopped, my breath catching. Because my office wasn't empty. Wait—no. It was empty of people, save me. It just had several non-human occupants making themselves at home on my desk.

A pair of plants.

The same flowers from the barbecue several weeks before.

"Oh, Smitty," I whispered, realizing that he must have planted one for me that day and kept it alive for me ever since.

I moved across the room, tracing my finger lightly over the velvet soft red petals. It was brightly colored and cheerful...and had a note tucked in beneath the leaves. Laughter bubbled up and out of my mouth when I realized the first one was Smitty's pot, and the note was instructions on the care and feeding of Bailey, his flower.

There was a postscript at the bottom, though, with an arrow to turn over the page.

And on the back was a cute drawing of the pair of us in cartoon form, hearts overhead, and the words,

BECAUSE SOMETIMES WINNING MEANS GETTING A LITTLE HELP.

"Aw, fuck," I breathed, my heart squeezing hard, a spark of something big and life-changing settling into my soul. I sat in that feeling for a second, sat in how good it made me feel, and then I set the drawing down and moved to the other flower, seeing that this one's name, written in glitter pen on the side of the ceramic pot, was Donner.

The man wasn't subtle.

But he was fucking wonderful.

Hands shaking, I reached for the package, unwrapped the cheerfully printed paper, opened the box, and smiled, my eyes prickling I was so touched.

A tiny unicorn sat inside, its expression a little grumpy, but in a cute way.

The mane was rainbow-colored fluff, threaded with glittery gold and silver strands, and its fur was so, *so* soft. Pulling it out, I cuddled it close, and noticed a piece of paper beneath, more of his slanted, compact writing scrawled across the page.

I'M HOPING THAT THIS ADORABLE GAL (NOTE THE LACK OF CREEPY, BEADY EYES) WILL REPLACE HERMAN IN HIS PLACE OF HONOR.

My eyes flicked to my monitor, where Herman had sat since that first day. Then went back to the note.

BUT I'M GUESSING THAT SHE WON'T, SO HOPEFULLY, AT THE VERY LEAST, SHE AND HERMAN WILL BE BEST FRIENDS.

P.S. IT MIGHT BE PRESUMPTUOUS, BUT I NAMED HER HAILEY.

Bailey, Hailey, Kailey. Conner, Donner.

I'd fucked up with Herman, needed to improve my rhyme game.

But, in fairness, Kailey was a bit easier to rhyme. What, was I going to rename Herman, Lonner? Tonner? Wonner?

Didn't quite flow off the tongue the same way.

The thought of names had me smiling, shaking my head at my ridiculousness, and picking up my phone, typing out a text.

> Just got into my office.

A few seconds brought a response.

> Oliver have the air on too cold again?

That had me laughing.

> No. But there were a couple of items on my desk.

A beat. A buzz.

> Extra work? I hate that.

I laughed again, shook my head. This *man.*

> Part of it is extra work.

Another buzz.

> And the rest of it?

My heart squeezed, a giant chunk breaking off, floating through space and time zones and over to a man who was quickly owning it. I posed the unicorn, snapped a picture, sent it over.

> Herman's got a new best friend.

The "..." appeared then disappeared. Then *reappeared*.

> Mean.

I grinned.

> Thank you, baby. Hailey made me smile, and the plants, don't worry, I'll keep them safe.

My phone vibrated.

> Then my day is complete.

That had my heart squeezing.

> Charmer.

Another buzz.

> Occasionally, but, little bird, I could give a fuck about the plants. I just wanted you to have a chance to participate if you wanted.

I typed back.

> I seem to remember a lot of heckling happening between you and the guys about who's going to win Mac.

Mac was the creepy blue monster that had been made purposely so-ugly-it-was-cute, and it had been the prize for the plant contest since their inaugural competition. I knew it brought bragging rights, especially amongst the very competitive professional athletes.

> Oh, if I win, I'm going to lay it on.

I shook my head.

> Well, I'll do my best to make sure that happens.

But before I hit send, I added,

> And if I kill Bailey, I'll happily accept my punishment.

A long pause. Then those dots did the reappearing, disappearing thing again.

> And now I'm desperately thinking of wombats so I don't have an erection in front of the guys.

My laughter was loud and bright and unembarrassed. Even a month ago, if I'd thought that I could be this comfortable in my own skin, laughing and bantering, even via text, with a man I loved—

Yes. *Loved.*

I sat in *that* for a second.

Realized it wasn't terrifying.

Maybe it should be.

Maybe I should run because it was too much too fast, but... it was me and Smitty. It was right, and...

Loved.

Yeah, I loved the man.

"You eat *THAT?*"

I had been reaching for the basket of mozzarella sticks (the cheese made in house, right along with the breadcrumbs), but the bitchy question had me freezing.

Yes.

Bitchy.

Because, frankly, Monica was a bitch.

A gorgeous, slender, beautifully contoured, and designer-clothes-wearing bitch.

And look, it wasn't the makeup *or* the designer clothes that Monica was sporting that made her a bitch.

Beth was equally put together (and thus significantly more put together than me and Pru, both in jeans, sneakers, T-shirts, and team hoodies). Hazel almost as much, looking gorgeous in her blouse and slacks, a pair of sensible flats on her feet and a pretty necklace to cap off the ensemble.

But there was a bit of drool on her shoulder.

Drool that Monica had sniffed at.

Monica, who was pregnant, and would soon be having a vomiting, drooling baby making a mess of all her designer digs.

That sniff, at someone I respected (Hazel was awesome and kind), had been the first strike.

The second had come after Beth had shown up, joining me, Pru, and Monica who had been waiting for her outside CeCe's (her flight had been late), when we'd walked into the bar.

Another sniff. A disgusted expression.

Daintily hefting her skinny ass onto the stool like it was climbing fucking Mount Everest, and then she'd touched the table—a worn and scuffed blond wood top—and made another face.

I'd caught Hazel's eyes then.

The psychologist's shoulders had risen and fallen on a sigh, but her expression had been bland, and she'd seemed determined that we would all have a good time, taking over the conversation and turning Monica's focus to what she clearly wanted to talk about.

Monica.

Pru had muttered something under her breath.

Beth's brows had dragged together.

But we joined in, and after a few minutes, the tension broke, and Monica, though centering the conversation constantly around herself, at least engaged with us, and it was with significantly less sniffing.

Though, there was snark (and a bit of sniffing when it came to ordering).

And snark about the paper napkins.

And snark about Julie, who the girls knew well and had served me and Smitty the other time I had been here. Julie, who was really nice and competent at her job, and definitely didn't deserve being sniffed at in disdain just because she'd asked Monica if she was sure that she only wanted a side salad for her entire meal.

Especially considering Monica had started off by declaring she was pregnant and the rest of us had ordered enough food to feed an army.

All of that could be forgiven.

Monica was a lot, but maybe she was just nervous and said the wrong thing (unlike me whose nerves meant I struggled to say *anything*).

But this?

Stopping me from eating one of the best things on the planet—fried cheese—and I was ready to snap, understanding be damned.

Hazel pushed the basket a little closer and smiled at me,

before flicking her gaze to Monica's and saying nicely, but firmly, "It's Cheese Night Extravaganza." She helped herself to a cheese stick. "You can have the salad you ordered, or any"—she swept a hand toward the copious baskets in front of us—"of this."

A protest welled in my throat because by this point in the evening I was feeling very possessive of my cheese, and Hazel offering it up to someone who might not appreciate it, seemed very sacrilegious.

But I bit my tongue.

Because God knew I didn't need to create drama for Raph, especially since he was going to marry this chick.

The irony didn't miss me either.

That I normally was desperate to talk, but that evening was struggling not to.

Smitty would get a kick out of that, and I couldn't wait to text him about this wild dinner, and how I'd suddenly become another person who kinda, sorta (okay, there was no *kinda, sorta* about it) wanted to dump a beer in Monica's lap, just to see how she'd react if her designer duds got ruined.

But drama.

I'd been around enough of it of my father's creation to want to avoid the entire process.

So, I just ate my cheese stick, soaked in the gloriousness of fried cheese, and when the guys' game came on TV, I devoted most of my attention to that.

I did manage to summon up a smile for Monica when she'd had enough of the attention being off her and onto the game and our respective men and prospects (Pru had two of the players she'd scouted playing that night and wanted to watch how they were doing, for obvious reasons, and Hazel always liked to watch how the guys were doing so that she could assess and help any who were struggling) and decided to leave.

This time it was less sniff and more huff, but I couldn't care less.

Because the moment that Monica had disappeared out the front door of CeCe's (let it be noted that it was without leaving any money to pay for her salad or the Diet Coke she'd ordered), Beth turned to the table and lifted a cheese stick like it was a sword.

"I hereby declare that she is never invited to Cheese Night Extravaganza again."

I, who was holding a tortilla chip that was—no surprise—doused in cheese (this of the bright orange, definitely not home-made but still delicious variety) froze as Beth whipped around to me and pointed that cheese stick right in my face.

"You, on the other hand, are faithfully invited to Cheese Night Extravaganza every week."

"Hear, hear," Hazel quipped.

Pru, who held a half-eaten cheese stick, gestured with it over her shoulder, eyes glued to the television that was playing the Breakers game. "I concur."

And I, fuck it, used that cheese stick to toast Beth's. "Good, because otherwise I think I'd show up anyway, and I promise that I'd make a dent in your cheese."

Hazel grinned.

Pru nodded approvingly.

Beth gave her another stick bump.

Then I stopped thinking about cheese and snarky women and focused on the game and the lovely, friendly group around me.

And just was.

No anxiety.

No drama.

Just being.

It was fucking perfect.

TWENTY-THREE

Smitty

I WAS LYING on the bed, still in my slacks, my suit jacket discarded to the side, my white button-down halfway unbuttoned.

And Kailey was talking my ear off, totally jazzed after her dinner out with Hazel, Pru, and Beth.

She'd glossed over the interactions with Monica, which had told me precisely how well they'd gotten on—that being not at all.

But then she'd talked about the girls and the food, and she'd watched me play—like she had every game since that first night together. Which made me feel about six feet—okay, *twelve* feet tall. It was fucking adorable hearing her talk about hockey, too, when she clearly still knew very little about the sport and said things like "quarters" and "the guy who played on the right side of the ice."

I'd never really been around someone who didn't know

much about hockey, let alone a woman who was interested in me, especially since I'd started playing for the Breakers.

The big leagues brought serious puck bunnies, but most of them—or at least the ones interested in me—knew that hockey had three periods and that right wing or right D was the person who'd been playing on that side of the ice.

If only because they needed to know when to go out to the parking lot and try to pick up the players...and which player to pick up.

Right.

So not the thing I needed to think about when my woman was talking to me on the phone.

"And I lost you," she said softly.

"Sorry," I said, "I'm just..." I sighed. "I was thinking about puck bunnies."

A pause. "What's that?"

I explained. "And I'm worried about Raph. He was..." Off wasn't the right word because he'd played well in the game, but there was something *off* about his mental state. Like something was wrong, but he wasn't sharing. "He's quiet," I finished lamely, which so wasn't a good explanation.

But the thing was, Raph wasn't a quiet guy.

He talked almost as much as me, and he was always playing pranks (hello, Herman), or at the very least, dishing out plenty of shit in the locker room.

"Because of Monica."

Not a question.

I sighed again. "Yeah, I think so, little bird."

"Maybe the pregnancy is really tough on her," she said. "I know that Hazel wasn't exactly loving the whole morning sickness beginning part."

"Yeah."

But it wasn't just that.

"But it's not only that," she said, agreeing with my inner worry.

"No." I blew out a breath and rolled to my stomach. "But I don't want to talk about that," I said, forcing the worry to the side, knowing that I wouldn't be able to do anything about it unless Raph let me in a little or he had a bit more clarity with what was going on.

"It's important to talk about the heavy stuff."

God, I loved this woman. "Yeah, it is," I agreed. "And we can do that more later. Now"—I hit the button for FaceTime—"I want to plan how I'm going to punish you."

The video connected, revealing her smiling face. "What have I done now, baby?"

"Oh, little bird, you've been a bad, bad girl."

EIGHT DAYS LATER—AND only not seven because I'd gotten home on the team's flight around three in the morning and didn't want to wake Kailey up—I was climbing the stairs to her apartment and finally going to see her in person.

FaceTime naughty time wasn't nearly as fun as real-life naked time.

We were very overdue for some naked time.

I needed to hold her, to taste her, to be inside her and—

Her door flew open.

And fuck, she was beautiful. Her smile, the way her face lit up, the blue dress that clung to her curves, her bare feet with pink-painted toes.

I clocked that all in a second.

Then she was in my arms and against my chest. Cinnamon in my nose, curves beneath my palms. *My* woman.

Home, even though I wasn't walking through my front door, but hers.

Home because she was pressed to me, or rather, because she was hopping up and I was lifting her as we moved inside, slanting our mouths together.

Her fingers clenched in my shirt, tugging me closer, tongue diving deep.

Her legs were tight around me.

Her moans were in my mouth.

It would be so easy to inch up the hem of her dress and— fuck it. It *was* easy, so I tugged up the bottom, slid my hands down and around and—

Fuck.

Her underwear wasn't more than a scrap of silk that left those plump, round cheeks bare. "Little bird," I murmured, breaking the kiss and carrying her into the kitchen.

"What?" she asked innocently, breathing hard.

"You've been naughty again."

"Because I put on clothes?" she asked silkily.

I dipped my finger under the thin strap that was sliding between her cheeks. "Is that what this is?" I asked, sliding it down, *down.*

She shivered as I plunked her on the kitchen counter, not bothering to tug down her dress. Yes, I'd had it all planned out, had wanted to take her out and—

Her hand came to my jeans, worked its way into the waist-band, fingers grazing the tip of my cock.

I needed her more.

Her dress was rucked up, baring miles of velvety skin, baring that tiny scrap of lace. Lavender. Sheer. Not concealing the small thatch of brown curls I'd kissed my way across many times over the last weeks, not concealing the plump folds of her labia, pink and glistening in the bright lights of the kitchen.

There was a little tie on that blue dress, something that must hold the two halves together, because while her clever little fingers of one hand worked at teasing the head of my cock, the other lifted, tugged at a slender strap of navy fabric.

And like fucking magic, the dress fell open.

A sheer bra revealing puffy pink nipples, the pouty tips calling for my mouth.

Hips that were a man's dream, something with substance, something to hold on to as I pounded deep.

A belly button that I'd dipped my tongue into, a trail of freckles I'd connected with my mouth, collarbones that seemed so slender and fragile and yet, if I kissed her there, if I flicked out my tongue, sucked the tender skin, her breath caught and her pussy dripped, and—

"Smitty," she whispered.

I'd been staring, because, fuck, she was gorgeous.

But she really wanted me to be doing.

So, I dropped to my knees, tugged the scrap of silk to the side, and fell onto her pussy. Tongue driving deep, mouth sucking hard, taking all the things I'd learned that she liked as we'd played and gotten to know each other and had moved slowly over the last weeks, and put them to good use.

This wasn't a war of delicate, careful touches and a slow surrender.

This was a war of breaking her apart with pleasure, making her shatter time and again, and then putting her back together.

Except, she surprised the shit out of me.

Because I felt her legs flex around me only a moment before she launched herself forward and off the edge of the counter, grinding her pussy against my mouth and making me stagger for a moment.

Then her hands were threading into my hair, holding me

tight. I had to react quickly so that she didn't fall backward, sliding my hands up her back and pressing her in.

Her hips bucked as I rose to my feet and spun, keeping her pussy against my mouth, continuing to work her as her legs wrapped around my shoulders, dangled down my back. I used leverage to pin her back against the cabinets, to get my mouth exactly where I wanted it, where she needed it, deeper and harder, tongue sliding into the hot, liquid depths and—

Her fingers clenched tight in my hair.

There.

Right fucking there. I kept working her, tongue thrusting and dragging up, pressing against her clit until—

She shuddered. Those fingers got tighter

"*Baby,*" she moaned, hips bucking as much as they were able, against my face. "I need you inside me."

"I am," I said, against her skin, and to prove my point, I thrust my tongue deeper.

Another tightening—this time her fingers *and* her tight, little muscles clenching around my tongue.

"Conner."

I opened my eyes, saw the sexiest thing I'd ever had the pleasure of viewing—pink cheeks, swollen lips, burning molten need blazing across emerald depths.

"Now, baby," she said. "Please."

And as if I could deny her anything.

A shift had her off my shoulders and resting on my chest, another had her down on her feet. I reached into my pocket for my wallet and the condom I had stashed there, but even as I had the plastic square out, she was unbuttoning my jeans, tugging down the zipper, freeing my cock.

Hot, wet lips on its length.

Suction that nearly sent me to my knees.

My hands were shaking when I tugged her off, when I tried to roll on the condom, when I lifted her again.

Too fast.

Too much.

But somehow her back was against the cabinets again, her legs around my hips this time, and the head of my cock was poised at her entrance.

For a second only.

Because then she was shifting down and I was thrusting up and then...

All that tight and wet and—fuck, but *tight*—heat was surrounding me.

Too fast. Too much.

Her head dropped back, and I barely managed to catch it before her skull collided with the cabinets, moans filling the air.

Slow. *Slow.* I needed to move—

A hand on my beard, drawing my focus to a burning green gaze. "Slow later, baby. Fast and hard now."

I was worried about hurting her.

I was worried about going too fast and scaring her.

I was—

She clenched around my cock, the ultimate feminine demand, and her nails dug lightly into my skin. "*Now*, honey."

And what was that about denying her anything?

Because it was impossible.

I moved, thrusting out and back in harder than I would have dared, *faster* than I would have dared, but her pussy was convulsing around me, her lips were parted, moans dripping off her tongue, hips meeting mine—

A shudder.

Me hitting just the right angle.

"*Fuck*," she groaned. "Fuck. Oh my God. Smitty. Oh—"

She'd never come with a man inside her.

I was going to be the one to make that happen.

That was the moment I stopped worrying about anything other than Kailey, her body, her reactions, the climax that was barreling her way. Thrusts at the angle that made her shudder, the rhythm that had pink darkening on her cheeks, the pressure that had sweat sheeting her body.

And then...

I saw her face change, saw the millisecond that things changed from good to almost there to going to happen and—

My name on her tongue, those eyes going wide, that pussy tightening around me.

She fell apart, and I was barely a moment behind her, my orgasm practically scorching the skin from my bones and turning me to ash.

I came out of it with my bare ass on her kitchen floor, her limp body in my lap, and the realization that—

"I didn't even get your underwear off, little bird."

Still.

Then laughter.

"Or your bra."

More laughter, so husky and soft that it had my cock still twitching and hard inside her, making it known that it was up for another round.

Her head tilted back; her lips curved. "Was that your punishment or mine?"

I didn't know.

I didn't care.

All I knew was that *now* the edge was off.

It was time for the war of delicate, careful touches, for her slow surrender.

And if that was my punishment, then I couldn't fucking wait.

TWENTY-FOUR

Kailey

A KISS to my wrist had my eyes opening, focusing after a few moments on the man curled up next to me in my bed.

I groaned and rolled over, backing myself against his frame, melting a little when his arm came around my middle, drawing me even closer to him. He was so big that his body dwarfed mine, that I could curl into him and find a safe harbor in the world.

Quiet.

Safe.

Peaceful.

Smitty.

"I'm debating," he said a few moments later, his chin moving lightly against my head as he spoke, the words ruffling my hair.

I waited for more, content to lie there with my eyes closed, languid and relaxed.

But when he didn't say anything further after a few moments, I prompted, "About what?"

He ran a hand down my side, up again, slow, slow trails of a roughly calloused palm prickling against my skin, making me shiver, my spine arch, hips bunching back against his pelvis. "Hmm?" he said, continuing the slow and steady motions.

It took a long time for me to process the query, to remember what I'd even asked, what he'd said.

Mostly because I had been fucked within an inch of my life.

But I was a fighter, and I got there in the end. "What are you debating?"

That hand drifted a little lower, stroking over my abdomen. "Ah," he murmured. "I had things planned."

I stilled, rolled to face him. "What do you mean?" I asked, staring up into his deep brown eyes.

"I mean," he said, "that before I saw you in that blue dress with the underwear that should be illegal"—a mock glare—"but is definitely for my eyes only—"

"I think we're about to test the limits of your appreciation for my sass, baby," I quipped, raising my brows.

"Or maybe yours for mine?"

A tug of his beard. "Precisely."

Grinning, that beard twitching, he leaned down and kissed me.

I loved that I could taste his smile on my tongue, feel it sweep through, settling into my bones. No, into my heart, as terribly cliché as that sounded. "Now," I said, that heart pounding when we finally broke apart, but I managed to pull it together enough to remember what had started this whole conversation.

And it wasn't my blue dress.

Or the barely-there lace I'd bought strictly for *his* eyes. *Not* that I would admit that…or that I'd nearly blushed myself into spontaneous combustion just buying them at the lingerie store. There was a reason I bought my toys online (discreet packaging anyone?) and not in person.

Not that I was ashamed.

But holy hell, having someone advise me on the recommended sexual pursuits of my vibrator had taken me about three levels beyond my comfort with that part of my life.

And…tangents.

Oh, so many tangents.

But I'd been learning that sometimes when I thought about comfort levels, a lot of the time it was my anxiety talking.

Be uncomfortable.

Be ashamed.

Be…wrong because I was *wrong* inside.

So maybe—

"Would you go to a vibrator class with me?" I blurted.

Which was *so* along that inner tangent and not close to asking Smitty what he had been debating that had drawn me out of my orgasm haze.

But his reaction was definitely worth the blush that chased my question.

His eyes went wide. His mouth dropped open. And then he did an impersonation of a goldfish that was both adorable and seriously hilarious considering it was happening on a six-foot-plus, two-hundred-twenty-pound professional hockey player's body.

"A *what?*"

I grinned, pushed him lightly so that he was on his back and I could clamber on top of him. "Not what you were debating?"

His eyes went hot. "There'd be no debating that, little bird."

My palms were on his chest, and I dragged my nails lightly down, trailing them over the faint notches of his abdomen. "So, you'd go?"

"Fuck no," he said.

I started, brows raising.

"I'd be teaching the fucking master class," he told me, voice going rough, hand lifting to cup my breast.

"Just for the record"—my breath caught when he brushed his thumb over my nipple—"that's not a vibrator."

A chuckle. He rolled it between thumb and forefinger. "I thought this was the *On* switch."

"It is." Laughter in my chest. "It definitely is."

That laughter cut off when he flipped us, and I suddenly found my back pressed into the mattress, the warm, heavy weight of him on top of me. Before I could protest or make another joke or redirect our conversation back to what he'd been debating, he kissed me.

And then I wasn't on mental tangents or worried about jokes or redirecting conversations.

I was focused on Smitty.

Because he made it impossible to do anything else.

A faint noise prickled at the edge of my consciousness, just as he was sliding down, his beard tickling me between my thighs, and I barely processed that it was my cell ringing before his tongue flicked out.

The rest of the world faded.

Just me.

Just him, and what he made me feel.

Which was so, so much.

"This isn't exactly what I had in mind," I said, as I looked up.

"Well, we missed the brunch reservations I made," he said, fingers laced through mine, "along with the movie I'd planned." A kiss to the tip of my nose. "*And* the dinner reservations. So"—he nodded at the dark trail ahead—"this is what we have left."

"A scary trail that should be on that creepy true crime documentary we watched earlier?"

A flash of white, his beard twitching in the way I loved.

Because *I'd* been the one to make him smile. *I* was the one who brought him joy. *I*—

An arm weaving around my waist, drawing me against him in a quick movement that stole my breath, bringing my flush against him. He pressed his mouth to the corner of mine. "Love this," he murmured, releasing me, and weaving our fingers together, drawing me forward again, tugging me along the manicured path.

"And I think the only thing we should continue to think about is how much better true crime is to baking shows to make love to."

I shook my head. "There's something seriously wrong with you."

A tap of his finger to his lips. "Or maybe it's the reality TV part and less about the actual content."

The man had a point.

The man also wasn't listening to me.

"Smitty." I dragged my feet. "I don't—"

His reaction was instantaneous, his big body stopping in a fraction of a second. He turned, releasing my hand, and crouched enough so that our faces were aligned. "Shit, little bird," he said, cupping my cheeks in those warm, calloused palms. "Is this too much? Do you need to stop? Are you feeling overwhelmed and—"

My heart squeezed so hard that for a moment I was unable to find words.

Not that they were stopped up in the back of my throat like when my anxiety was gripping me and it felt like I couldn't breathe, couldn't think, couldn't move or speak or even exist sometimes.

But the words didn't come because I was so fucking touched that he'd react like that.

That he'd stop and check in with me.

Not push on and tell me to power through because we were doing this.

Not caring that the effort he'd put into planning this would be for naught if I *couldn't* do it, and—

He shifted minutely, the worry creasing his face, and I realized that he didn't know the reason for my silence and was probably thinking that it was for the worst possible reason, that I was falling apart inside, unable to interact and—

Still, there was patience in his demeanor.

Worry, yes, but he'd wait. Wait all fucking day if he had to.

And that unstuck me.

I moved closer, rising on tiptoe and pressing my mouth to his. I hugged him tightly, wanting to impart everything I was feeling onto him, wanting him to know, to understand exactly how much him reacting that way meant to me.

"Smitty," I whispered, and his eyes locked with mine. All the words swirled within me, stuck and not, pressing against me, desperate to get out. And eventually they did. "I love you," I said, my hand on the warm skin of his cheek, the soft bristles of his beard tickling my palm. "I love you, and it's not too much. I don't need to stop. Not with you. Not *ever* with you."

He sucked in a breath, spine going ramrod stiff. "Little bird," he croaked, his hand covering mine. "Little bird, I love you so fucking much."

Now it was my turn to hold still, to inhale sharply. Those words.

They were as good as his arms wrapping around me.

And under the rustling leaves of the trees overhead, the faint glimmer of the stars in the sky, the creepy as hell dark trail behind us, he held me tightly, those words between us, I felt light and fresh and new and unbroken.

I felt *whole*.

Myself.

Then I shivered, and Smitty seemed to unstick, one arm shifting, wrapping around my shoulders, the other dropping to his side.

He started walking, but instead of guiding me toward the dark and creepy trail, he turned us, towing me to the parking lot.

"What about your trail?" I asked, heels digging in again.

"It's a trail with a kickass view," he said, "but it's a trail that's not going anywhere, little bird."

"But"—I glanced back—"we're here already and—"

A flex of movement, his body bending and straightening as he scooped me up against his chest. "You just told me you love me." His eyes blazed into mine. "I'm not taking you on a serial killer trail. I'm taking you home."

Home.

That was absolutely perfect.

TWENTY-FIVE

Smitty

I WAS SITTING on her little blue couch—so *little* it was almost comical trying to fit my big body on it, even without Kailey beside me—a beer in my hand, a Gold game on TV.

Watching Brit Plantain in net was incredible, especially since rumor had it that she'd be retiring when her contract was up in two years.

Having played against her many times in both of our long tenures in the league, I knew that she was legit one of the toughest goalies I'd ever played against. This was mostly because she was extremely agile and a hard worker. If there was a weakness in her game, she didn't rest until it was remedied.

She had the best goals against average in the league. The highest save percentage.

And it had been that way for three years.

But her husband, and former captain, Stefan Barie, had retired several years back, and they'd recently adopted an adorable little girl named Roxie, and were planning on expanding their family.

Stefan was playing the stay-at-home dad and rocking that shit if the video feed of him cradling their baby in decked out Gold gear, a sparkling golden bow on her peach-fuzz-covered head was any indication, but I understood the urge to not be away from the family for half the year, especially when Brit had played in the league for as long as she had.

I lived and breathed the sport.

But if I had kids at home, it would be hard as hell to leave them behind.

I didn't envy Raph.

Gotta get that big-league money before we retired, though.

Play it smart, retire on top, live happily ever after.

That was *my* plan, anyway. And Brit was smart enough to have a plan of her own, so I was just going to enjoy the magic— be proud as fuck that we'd managed to eke out four wins against them in the finals to take home the Cup and enjoy feeling domestic.

Because I was by myself on that tiny couch, that beer in hand, the game in hand, and Kailey was working on her computer.

She'd shyly asked if I minded her working on a side project for a few hours, since she was close to being done, and I'd told her the truth.

I didn't mind at all.

We'd come back to her place the night before, stayed up for hours worshipping each other's bodies, and every time she'd told me she loved me, I had felt a little jolt in my body. I would never *ever* get tired of her saying those words to me.

So today, when we'd woken up late, with a day off for me, and it being the weekend for her (off minus her side projects that was), I hadn't been in any hurry to move.

We'd lazed in bed.

We'd showered together.

We'd ordered in lunch and cuddled on that small ass couch. And then Kailey had gone to her computer, and I'd caught up on some shows, unable to resist the urge to glance at her at regular intervals, to watch her work, her fingers moving furiously on the keyboard, her eyes glued to the screen. Totally transfixed and in the zone.

For hours.

It was fascinating.

She was amazing.

I could never find that kind of stillness in myself, always moving—my leg bouncing or tossing a ball when off the ice, or when on it, shooting a puck, working on my edges, flexing my stick. Even studying tape had to be done on the treadmill.

In fact, the only time I'd found stillness was with Kailey.

Talking to her.

Holding her.

Even just being here in this apartment.

I didn't think I could sit at a computer for six hours, though, even if she wanted to play that dragon game she'd shown me before she'd begun working.

Cool game.

Something I'd definitely be down for, at least for a few hours.

But I didn't have the patience to sit down and muddy my way through programming.

Thankfully, I had a really smart girlfriend who *was* good at it.

So, I'd left her to her project, cleaned up the food from lunch, washed the sheets we'd made a mess of because we'd eaten in bed and got crumbs everywhere (not to mention our activities of the previous day and last night), and remade the bed. Then I'd searched her cabinets, found enough in them to make a simple meal of a salad and pasta, unfreezing some garlic bread, and somehow managing to not burn it.

I'd made her a plate, brought her that and a beer, placing both on her desk and earning myself a slightly dazed smile, her pretty green eyes blinking up at me.

"You need me to stop?" she asked, the work haze beginning to leave her face.

"No," I murmured. "Just...sustenance. Can't have you wasting away."

She snorted, but smoothed her hand over my cheek, my beard in that way that never failed to make my heart skip a beat. "With *this* body?"

Slowly I'd spun her chair, planted my palms on her thighs. "I know you're not talking shit about yourself, little bird. I happen to love this body."

A smile, that other hand coming up to join the first on my face. "You've shown me that, and I like my body. It's strong. It's capable. It..."

"Gives you orgasms so long as you're watching reality TV?"

Laughter in her eyes. "I thought you were responsible for those."

"Nope," I said, playing innocent. "It was the vibrator class."

That sent the laughter from her eyes and onto her tongue, filling the air with the soft, melodic sound of her amusement.

"Eat, little bird," I'd ordered before I could distract her further, "Or I'll have to punish you again."

More humor. Another smile that hit me right in the solar plexus. "Now you're just tempting me."

She'd been tempting *me*.

But I'd managed to just press a kiss to her lips (and keep it relatively short) then had retreated to the couch, turning occasionally to make sure she was eating.

When she'd finished, I'd retrieved the plate, soaked in some hockey and the very talented Brit Plantain, and just enjoyed the domesticity, the stillness, the settling of being with her, even though we weren't doing the same thing.

"Baby?"

I blinked, realized I'd been daydreaming and the game had gone to intermission while I'd been thinking about all things that were my wonderful, perfect woman, and meanwhile had missed that my *wonderful, perfect woman* was approaching.

Her hair was piled on top of her head, and she had those tortoiseshell frames perched on her nose, the smattering of freckles beneath them and polka dotting the bridge and the tops of her cheeks.

But it was her hands that had me blinking away the relaxed fog the day had brought.

They were wringing together.

Fingers woven and sitting just beneath her belly button, as though trying to contain something—butterflies? Nerves? A creepy monster that would burst out a la *Alien* (though, for the record, I'd still love her, even *with* a baby alien inside her).

The skin of her hands was turning white and pink as her fingers squeezed and released, her fingers shifting along each other, clenching and relaxing.

I placed my palm over the top of her hands, stilling the movement, stopping her from hurting herself. "What do you need, little bird?"

Nerves and excitement in emerald eyes. "Can I show you something?"

On my feet in a second, my palm going to the side of her neck. "Of course, honey."

"Right." A breath. Her chin went up, shoulders straightened. "It's over here," she said, turning away and leading me to her computer. When I made it there, she placed a hand on my arm. "Will you sit?"

I sank down into her chair, let her roll me close.

"I—" A breath. "I made this for you thinking it'd be helpful, but now I'm worried that you might be upset because you don't need it and it's presumptuous, and I didn't mean to make it seem like you *needed* it and—"

"Little bird," I said, covering her hand. "I won't be mad, I promise."

"Right." She inhaled again. "Okay, so I was thinking about your dyslexia and how it's a struggle sometimes"—her eyes flicked to mine—"not that you can't manage it and—"

"Honey."

She swallowed. "Right," she whispered. "So, I was thinking that this might help." Leaning forward, Kailey brought her hand to the mouse, clicked the button. "So, I made this." Teeth into her lip. "It's just a simple plug-in, but if you click this"—another press on the mouse—"then it'll take the text on the page and change it into one of the open-source dyslexia fonts that are supposed to make it easier to read."

I went still.

She kept talking. "There are a few different fonts, and I didn't know if you had a preference, so I just picked the ones with the best reviews and—"

I looked at the page in front of me.

It was about her game.

And I could see that—*read* that—without a struggle.

The pile of hair on her head tipped precariously when she turned back to me. "And it's totally something that you don't have to use if—"

She'd made it for me. She'd made *this* for *me*.

For. Me.

"—you don't want to and—"

She squeaked.

Because I tugged her down into my lap, wrapping my arms around her tightly—too tight probably—but fuck if my eyes weren't burning as I buried my face into her throat, holding her to me and trying to breathe through the emotion that was so thick it was choking me.

"Smitty," she whispered after several long moments. Then, "Baby" after several more.

I lifted my head, let her see what she'd done to me.

That hand on my cheek.

Her expression was soft. "You like it," she whispered.

"I love it," I said. "I don't think anyone has ever done anything more thoughtful for me."

"Really?" Her brows dragged together.

"Really."

"That's not right," she told me, that frown deepening. "You deserve so much, baby. You deserve everything."

"Fuck."

More frowning.

"Now I need to kiss you."

The frown smoothed. "And that's a problem?"

"It's a problem because I want to use it and I want to hear how you made it and I want to say thank you so fucking much because it is the most incredible thing someone has done for me, but instead, I'm going to kiss you and then I won't be able to say all of that and—"

Her lips hit mine.

And I found that I could show my gratitude without words.

***

LOUD KNOCKING WOKE me many hours later.

My eyes snapped open, I shot up to sitting, my gaze shot to the door of Kailey's apartment.

It was vibrating like it was going to fly off its hinges.

"What the—"

Next to me, Kailey gasped and sat up.

At the same time, her phone began blowing up.

"—fuck?" I finished, the pounding not relenting.

Kailey grabbed her cell. I tossed back the blankets, headed for the door.

"Wait," Kailey said.

But I was already looking through the peephole, seeing that an older guy in a suit was the one doing the knocking. He had one arm in the air, fist pounding against the door. The other was at his ear, holding a phone.

Seriously. What. The. *Fuck?*

I whipped open the door.

The man had his fist raised, ready to knock again, and the incredulous expression on his face as he took me in, who for what it was worth, probably should have tugged on a pair of underwear before opening the door.

But I hadn't, and we were here now and—

"Who are you?" Disdain in the question, the incredulity that had been present for a moment as he'd presumably been taking in a six-foot, two-hundred-twenty-pound man standing naked in the doorway.

"Why the fuck are you pounding on my girlfriend's door in the middle of the night?"

A flick down, back up. Brows lifting. "Your *girlfriend's?*"

A hand on my side, and then Kailey was pressing into me, her robe belted tight. "Dad," she said, and there was definite frost in her tone.

Frost that was fucking Antarctica in my body as I realized

this man, showing up and acting like this in the middle of the night, was the one who'd wounded Kailey so deeply.

"What are you doing here?" she asked, leaning a little heavier against me.

"You didn't pick up your phone."

As though that were explanation enough.

A door down the hall cracked open, an older woman peeking her head out. "Kailey? Is everything"—her eyes flicked down, and I doubly realized that my comfort with being naked hadn't served me well in this situation—"okay?" she finished slowly.

"We're fine, Bernie," Kailey called. "Sorry to disturb you." A flick of her eyes to her father. "Wh-why don't you come in and we can talk about this?"

A flicker of nerves.

I slid my hand down her back.

Her father huffed, but when Kailey opened the door a little wider, allowing her dad entry, he moved into the apartment.

"Okay?" I murmured, taking her hand and drawing her toward the bed. My underwear had to be somewhere in the vicinity.

A shake of her head had my heart clenching.

Fuck.

"I'm here," I whispered. "I'll make it okay."

"I know," she whispered back. "But he's—"

Her gaze went across the room, where her father was glaring, arms crossed, his impatience palpable and almost whip-like.

"—he can be really...mean." The last almost inaudible.

There.

My underwear was halfway under the foot of the bed.

I tagged it, dragged it up my legs. Then I wrapped my arm

around her shoulder, tucking Kailey close, and went to face the fucking dick who was pacing across the rug in her living room.

She was trembling, but she still managed to ask. "Why did you come?"

Her father's expression soured further. "I told you—"

"I didn't answer my phone?" she interrupted, nails biting into my side. "That doesn't explain why you flew across the country and invaded my apartment in the middle of the night."

"You're my only daughter." A snapped-out response. "And it's incredibly disrespectful to be questioning me when I'm only concerned for your well-being."

"I-I didn't answer for twenty-four hours, and instead of waiting like a normal person for a response, you took the jet and—"

"Wanted to make sure you were okay?" His volume increased, and Kailey flinched.

"You sh-should have—"

Venom in his tone that had her flinching again. "I should have *what exactly?*"

And *that* was enough.

I shifted, tucking Kailey behind me. "You need to go."

Her father rocked back slightly. "Excuse me?"

"You're acting like an asshole and scaring your daughter." Rage roiled across the father's face, but I pressed on. "If you want to be in her life"—fuck that, but I wouldn't deny Kailey anything, not even this—"then you need to get your shit together, come back at a reasonable time with a better fucking attitude."

"And who the fuck are you?" her father snapped.

"I'm the man who loves your daughter and won't stand by while she gets abused."

A vein flickered in her father's forehead, but he didn't say anything, just spun on his heel and strode toward the door, whipping it wide. He turned back on the threshold, bypassing me completely, his gaze moving to Kailey's, who'd sidled forward slightly and was glued to my side. "Next time I call, pick up the phone."

The order brought another tremble through her body.

"She'll decide when and where to answer her calls," I said.

Cold green eyes coming to mine.

I stood my ground.

Then her father was through the door, the heavy panel slamming loudly behind him.

Moving quickly, I drew Kailey close as I locked the door then lifted her into my arms as I strode back to bed. Blankets up and over her. Arms wrapped tight.

But her trembles were intense, only growing stronger.

So, I held tighter and waited long minutes, practicing patience even though my insides were clawing at me to do something, to chase after that fucker and help him understand what an NHL player's fist felt like.

But I was learning that sometimes the strongest thing I could do was to be still, be silent, be *there*.

And eventually, her shaking subsided.

Eventually, her gaze met mine. "I'm sorry," she whispered.

"For what?" I asked, stroking my fingers through her hair.

"I-I—" A breath, her lids sliding closed then opened. "Every time he's like that, I can't say anything. I just stand there and—"

"Baby," I said, hating to interrupt her, but she needed to know.

"What?" Her eyes drifted away, shame in those emerald depths.

"*You* participated in that conversation. You held him

accountable—or tried to, anyway. Did he listen? Fuck no, he didn't." I tilted her head back. "But you weren't silent, little bird. You were strong, and you communicated your thoughts and—"

"I didn't tell him to leave, didn't get him to go out the door."

Ah.

That was what this was about.

"That's my job, little bird," I said. "I'm big and strong and good at scaring people and hitting shit"—her brows dragged together—"I'm good at being the one doing the enforcing, and I don't mind taking your back when you need it."

Still. Her body went still.

Then it relaxed, her hand coming to my cheek, my jaw.

"Big and strong," she murmured, and hell if I didn't feel that right in my cock. "But what happens when you're not strong, baby?" she asked. "What happens when you need *me* to be the enforcer, and I struggle to step up in the same way?"

First, that would never happen.

Second, that would never happen.

But...

"You helped me with Hazel's shit," I said. "And you made the plug-in for me. You found ways to care for me and"—I smiled, really wanting to lighten the mood so that I could either get my woman the rest she needed, or to get my woman off—"I doubt that you'll stop finding them. Plus," I added, "I think we both know that strength doesn't always pair with size or the ability to make a scene."

"Oliver," she whispered.

I nodded.

My friend, who'd lost his leg and rebuilt his life without seeing it as a loss.

"And Pru," she added.

Another nod. The scout had experienced her share of childhood trauma, but she'd made a great life for herself.

"And others."

I pressed my lips to her forehead.

"And *you*, little bird. You're the strongest person I know."

TWENTY-SIX

Kailey

"ANOTHER CHEESE STICK, MADAME?" Beth asked, two weeks later, on what was becoming our bimonthly Cheese Night Extravaganza.

I passed her the basket, and Beth swooped in and helped herself to the yummy fried cheese. I made a mental note to add in a few walks around the block to compensate for the extra calories I consumed on these evenings.

"We're thinking about adopting."

Pru.

My breath caught, feeling too new to this group to be part of this conversation, but also touched that they had accepted me so easily.

Beth set down her cheese stick, reached over, and covered Pru's hand. "I meant what I said at the wedding"—which had happened over the summer; I had been invited, but was so new and gripped by my anxiety I obviously hadn't attended—"I will carry your babies."

Pru inhaled sharply, turned her palm over and squeezed her friend's hand. "I know you meant it. I just..." Another breath. "I don't think I'm there yet."

Beth nodded. "Okay, honey. But if you do..."

Pru smiled, squeezed again, and then grabbed her beer, taking a long swallow. "It's a long process to adopt," she said, "so I have time to get over the rest of the nerves."

Pru? Nerves?

"How?"

I didn't realize I'd asked that aloud until three heads swiveled my way. "Sorry," I said, lifting my hands. "I just—" A shake of my head. "Never mind, it doesn't matter. Tell me about the process. What do you and Marcel have to do?"

Pru's head tilted to the side. "Paperwork. Attorneys." A beat. "Now, what do you mean *how?*"

I bit my lip, glanced to Hazel for help.

The psychologist merely raised her brows.

"How do you have nerves?" I whispered. "You just seem so"—a wave of my hand—"together and confident, and I'm—" I broke off. Struggled.

"Not?" Pru finished.

A shrug. A nod. My eyes on My cheese.

The table went quiet, the only sounds that of CeCe's around us—the loud hum of conversations, the *clink* of silverware and plates and cups.

Then a warm, strong hand on mine.

"You're fucking great, Kailey," she said. "Smart and pretty, and you have this quiet strength that I envy."

I frowned.

"Sometimes it's impossible for me to sit and be quiet. I'm always chasing a high and for years, I used that high of life to hide all the shit in my life."

"But you're so strong."

Pru's smile gentled. "Is it? To be constantly running instead of living?"

"What about constantly hiding instead of living?" I asked and glanced across the table, happening to catch Beth's eyes. "Because that's what I've done."

Beth's face changed, a flicker here and gone, but then Hazel spoke.

"*Is* that what you've done?"

A breath. "No," I said, "it's not quite that simple."

"Right."

"But it still feels weak, especially when I can't even stand up to my dad, and he's awful, and now I'm supposed to meet Smitty's parents, and they're not like my family. They're *good*."

He'd asked the previous night.

His family was coming to town.

Supposedly, they were more than good. Supposedly, they were great.

And all I'd been able to do since agreeing to have dinner with them was panicking—because I *had* to meet his family—but my dad was...my dad, and my mom hadn't shown any interest in my life in *years,* and Smitty's family was involved in his life, and what if I couldn't talk and was frozen in my own damned mind and—

What if they didn't like me?

Hazel leaned forward. "Want to tell me why that's scary?"

"Oh no," Pru said. "I've got *that* one. It's terrifying because they're part of him, and maybe they'll have their faults, but you want them to like you despite *your* faults, and then it's just this scary cycle of faults and panic and wanting to make a good impression and—" A wave of her hand. "It's just shit. All around, but you'll get through it, especially if they love Smitty. He loves you, so they'll love you."

"That seems like an oversimplification," Beth said. "Just

saying," she added when Hazel and Pru glared at her. "I mean *I* know you're great, but families are complicated, and it's...just not always that simple."

Yeah.

It seemed like that, too.

Hazel leaned across the table and squeezed my hand. "You know Smitty," she said. "You see how protective he is of the guys, of you. Do you have any doubt that he would tolerate anything less than full acceptance of our girl?"

Pru shook her head. "No. Absolutely not."

Beth paused, considered that. "I don't know him all that well, but you make a good argument, Haze."

Hazel whispered out of the side of her mouth. "That's as close to an agreement as we'll get from our corporate exec, Beth."

I giggled.

Because agreement from Beth or not, Hazel did make a good point, and Pru did, too, even if it was a bit too rose-colored glasses for me, considering my brain tended toward worst case scenario.

But the truth was, this came down to me and Smitty.

To what we had together and what we were building for the future.

And I knew that Smitty *would* protect me.

The only thing that scared me was not being able to protect him back.

My stomach churned.

My throat was tight.

I felt like I was walking toward the guillotine—if that came in the form of three people who loved and cared for the man that *U* loved and cared for.

This should be easy.

But like things often were in my life, it wasn't all that easy. It was complicated and difficult and something I had to force myself to do, just hoping that I'd get through and it would get easier and—

Fingers on my cheek. "It'll be okay," he said. "I promise."

"What if I can't talk?" I whispered.

"Then you'll be quiet and mysterious, and they'll be desperate to get together with you again so that they can get to know the beautiful woman with all the mysterious secrets."

A roll of my eyes. "Or they'll want to run from the woman who's a bitch and standoffish."

"No, little bird. That's not you. Even when you're quiet, you're still warm."

"How about when I told you I wasn't interested."

He grinned, nipped my nose. "Still warm."

"And when I ran from the party?"

A press of his mouth to mine. "Still warm."

"And—"

A deeper kiss, tongue dipping in and tangling with mine.

"Baby," I began when he pulled back. "I—"

His eyes sparked with amusement, but he merely swiped a thumb across my lips and straightened, saying, "Oh hey, Mom."

And I died.

Right there.

Just a little.

I HAD a drink in my hand—and one in my belly—and it made things slightly better.

At least with alcohol the memory of turning and seeing Smitty's mom behind me, an indulgent smile on her face, had faded slightly.

My heart had still been racing, my legs shaking just the littlest bit, and then I'd had to introduce myself and make small talk until Smitty's dad and brother had returned from parking the car.

Celeste had a broken foot, a cane, and a sense of humor that rivaled Smitty's, joking that she'd break the other foot if it meant she'd get curbside service, and hearing that, seeing the easy smile that was like Smitty's, the sparkling brown eyes that were so similar to her son's, and the tension had eased inside me.

No spinning blades, whirling machetes slicing through me.

Just a bit of shy and following Smitty's lead.

Which had been as it always was—patient and easy-going.

So, by the time his dad and brother came, the blades stayed sheathed, and I was able to stay relaxed...relatively anyway.

Ryan, Smitty's dad, was a little quiet. Not standoffish, but seemingly just used to Smitty and Celeste dominating the conversation. Brandon, his brother, was quiet as well, but...he kind of gave me a weird vibe.

Like...there was some tension under the surface I couldn't comprehend.

Nothing overt.

Nothing terrible.

Just...something that was rubbing and uncomfortable and might eventually cut through to the surface. And in the meantime, it was all just—

There.

Barely-healed over.

"Here you go," Julie said, sliding a plate of food in front of Celeste. "The daily special with tomato soup." A shift of movement brought food to me (I'd laid off the cheese and gone for wings), and then the guys' burgers were off the large tray Julie had perched on her shoulder and dispersed to their proper locations.

"Thanks, Jules," I said, having gotten to know the server, at least a little bit, considering how often I'd been into CeCe's.

The other woman smiled and gave me a sly high-five as she mouthed, "You got this."

And so far, I had.

The nerves meant I wasn't completely comfortable, not like I was with Smitty or my friends (yes, somehow *I* had friends), but it wasn't like I was sitting on my stool, feeling like a writhing uncomfortable bundle of anxiety.

"This is delicious," Celeste said, spooning up some soup.

"For such a dingy-looking place, the burger's good," Brandon said, and I froze, my wing poised in front of my lips, feeling almost defensive of CeCe's.

Was it marble and glass and a Michelin-starred restaurant? No.

But it was homey and warm, and they made good food, had a friendly staff, and...I could be myself here.

My eyes narrowed slightly, but I decided to ignore the comment, as I had with the weird vibe and the other couple of snarky replies Brandon had given that evening, following Celeste and Ryan's lead and focusing on my wings and my beer. My eyes hit Smitty's—who smiled tightly and took a bite of his burger—his knee brushing mine, silently telling me that it was okay. I nodded slightly. Then Ryan asked me about my job with the Breakers. Giving him my standard rundown of the program meant that I was distracted from the comment, and add in Celeste asking about my family, and the verbal tap-dance of that topic of conversation—"My dad works a lot, and we're not close. My mom is really busy with her charities. I don't have any brothers or sisters."

Bare facts.

Enough that I hopefully wouldn't have to get into it in further detail.

At least not today.

Luckily, it seemed to satisfy his parents because the conversation then turned back to the team (and I didn't miss that Smitty was the one doing the slight redirecting, just another reason I loved the man).

They were talking about the season and the prospects for what might happen when the playoffs rolled around when Brandon struck again. "Yeah, it's lucky that Conner managed to squeak into the NHL. He was so bad at school that he wouldn't have had a backup plan."

Celeste gasped.

Brandon smiled, and it was tinged with the jealously that coated his words, which was obvious to me now. "Probably be working at McDonald's now if he hadn't."

"*Brandon,*" Ryan snapped.

Like working in the service industry was bad.

Like *Smitty* was bad and a disappointment and stupid.

Like his biggest worry he'd worked to bury deep.

And his brother was just poking it with a sharp stick.

Smitty winced, but his voice was calm. "Look, Brandon, man. Let's not do this now. We're having a nice dinner, and you don't need to ruin it with old shit."

Brandon's eyes narrowed. "You took my spot."

Celeste and Ryan stilled.

Smitty sighed. "This was more than a decade ago, Brand, and you know I had no control over who got chosen—"

"Chosen?" I asked.

"*He* took it," Brandon snapped, his eyes flashing to mine.

"He took *my* spot on the team, and if I'd had it, I would be here instead of where I'm at and—"

"Brandon," Ryan interjected. "You know—"

"Oh, *I* know. I know how *proud* you are of him and how *I'm* just the normal one— You know he's dyslexic, right?" he asked, still staring at me. "Was so fucking dumb in school that he barely passed. A disappointment to his teachers. Hell, Mom and Dad had to get him a ton of tutors and—"

"*Brandon,*" Celeste snapped.

Was a thirty-year-old man seriously saying these things?

Rage built in my belly, flickered up and out through my limbs.

My throat spasmed.

I glanced at Smitty, saw his face had gone pale, his expression stark.

"You're seriously holding a grudge about not making a team years ago?" I asked, bracing when Brandon's gaze whipped to mine, lips parting. "And is where you are now so bad?" A swallow. "You know what Smitty told me before we came to dinner? How proud of you he is," I said before he could interject. "He was so freaking excited that you just got the job at a Fortune 500 company, talked my ear off about how proud he was of you."

The venom began to leak out of Brandon's face.

But I wasn't done.

The words kept coming.

"And this night, when you're meeting me, something he's excited to share. Not that I'm this amazing treasure—"

"You are."

I glanced to the side, saw Smitty's eyes glimmering.

"You are," he said again.

"You are, too," I whispered, reaching forward and covering his hand with my own. "And you're smart and funny and the man I love." I glanced back at Brandon. "So, before you start bringing up shit that should have been left in the past more than ten years ago, you should think about the kind, generous man who's sitting here with us, of his pride in you." A breath. "And you should consider that he might worry about his own worth, about all those things you mentioned as faults, about being a disappointment, and how hard he works to *not* be one." My eyes narrowed. "Because, for some damned reason, he wants to impress you."

Brandon was ghost white.

But I pressed on.

"Then you should think about who the real disappointment is."

TWENTY-SEVEN

Smitty

"EXCUSE ME," Kailey said, releasing my hand and hopping down from her barstool.

A second later, she was hurrying across the bar floor, disappearing down the hall.

Her disappearing out of sight had me finally unsticking.

My feet hit the floor, and I started after her when my mom caught my arm.

"We'll take care of the bill. And"—her face clouded—"your brother. Will you ask Kailey if we can try this again? Promise her that it'll be without a side of the bullshit?"

I took a breath, released it slowly. "Yeah, Mom."

Her hand hit the side of my neck, squeezed lightly. "Also, for the record, you should marry the girl."

My lips turned up. "Already planning on it."

"I'm—" A squeeze before she released my hand. "I've never been disappointed in you, baby," she whispered. "I know you have to go after your girl, but I need you to know that I've always loved you for the man you are. The kind, selfless, bright, and wonderful person you are defines you, not how easily you can read some letters on a page."

Shit.

Now my eyes were burning.

My stare caught my dad's as I moved from the table, snagging Kailey's jacket and purse. "Go," my dad mouthed, "we'll talk later."

"I—" Brandon began.

"Not fucking doing this right now, man," I said.

I turned away from my brother, wove across the floor, moved into the hall. Jules was coming around the corner as I entered it.

"Out the back door."

"Thanks, Jules."

My legs made quick work of the hall, and then I was pushing out into the night air.

Kailey was there, her face in her hands.

It was cold, so I dropped her jacket around her shoulders, tugged her close, and just held her. Those hands stayed on her face, but she burrowed into me, letting me hold her.

Long minutes later, she asked, "Did I really say all that?" A whispered question. "Or was it just a bad dream and I'm going to wake up, go to dinner with your parents and be the perfectly charming girlfriend and—"

"I love you."

She stilled.

"My fierce little bird, pecking the eyes out of the person who tried to hurt me."

Those hands dropped to my chest.

Her eyes finally hit mine.

"He made me mad."

One half of my mouth kicked up. "He made me wish we were on the ice so I could check him through the boards."

A breath, her forehead falling forward.

I dropped my hand to her nape, held her there, was lightly massaging the tight muscles there.

"I fully support this idea," she murmured.

That made me want to laugh. When I really shouldn't want to after what happened inside CeCe's. So, I held it back and just hugged her tightly until she stopped trembling, until she relaxed against me. "My fierce little bird," I said again, stroking a hand down her spine.

I felt her smile against my skin. "I'm not going to hear the end of this, am I?" she asked softly.

"Definitely not," I told her.

"They'll hate me."

Fingers in her hair, tilting her head back. "My mom just told me to marry you."

She started, going completely still, mouth dropping open.

"For the record, I told her I'd already planned on it."

Her exhale was shaky. "Smitty."

"This isn't a proposal," I said, smoothing my thumb over her bottom lip, "though I'm not saying that I wouldn't elope if you gave me the chance."

"No."

I frowned.

"I want the wedding," she whispered. "I want everyone to see how much I love you."

For the second time in less than an hour, I was near tears. "I love you so fucking much," I whispered, "and I'm so thankful, so proud of you for what you said, for being here, being in my life and—"

My voice cracked.

I pushed on. "For never making me feel like a disappointment."

A hand on my cheek, brushing lightly against my beard. "Baby."

I smiled. "Thanks for standing up for me." A breath. "I clearly have some things to unpack with them. I...Brandon has done shit like that before, and I've always laughed it off. Never to that point," I added. "Never that overt. But, yeah, he's made the occasional sharp or snarky comment."

"Maybe he saw you were happy and couldn't take it."

"Maybe." But it seemed like more than that, more than just being jealous, and I didn't know what to do with that.

Brandon was my older brother.

I'd always looked up to him.

Wanted to be like him.

To think that Brand had fostered this *antipathy* for years made me feel off-balanced.

Wrong.

Despite my mom's assurances. Despite what Kailey said.

If my *brother* could think those things about me...then who else might?

"Baby?" Kailey whispered.

I blinked, pushed the question away. "It's cold. Let's get out of here and go home."

A flex of her fingers, but her hand slid away, drifted down, and wove with mine. "Yeah, baby, let's go home."

I WENT OUT with my parents for breakfast the next morning.

Brandon had flown home early, and I was glad I hadn't had to deal with my brother, not when I felt both settled because I fucking loved Kailey for speaking up for me when I knew how difficult it was for her, and that she'd done it for *me*...yeah, that fucking *slayed* me.

But I was supremely rattled.

I hadn't known my brother had that much dislike for me, disdain for my abilities.

My parents had made it clear they were proud of me, and I hated that a part of me had needed those words, that they'd been like water to a parched desert. It wasn't like they'd ever shirked on praise, and it concerned me that part of me needed that praise, especially since I was a fucking adult.

Maybe that wasn't fair.

Maybe people always needed that from their parents.

Maybe so much had shifted in my mind in the last months that I needed that, especially now.

Lots to think about when I should be focusing on hockey.

I'd asked Kailey to come for part of the road trip. The team would be going to some big cities, places that would make for fun nights out. There were a few restaurants I'd love to take her to, ones I'd found on my walks through the cities, little hole-in-the-wall places and underrated tiny bistros with the best fucking food.

But Kailey couldn't come.

She'd been working on that side project for Marcel's dad in her spare time and was nearly done, so she'd decided to pass on the road trip, promising to get it done, so we'd spend my free weekend when I got back from the travel together.

I had *plans* for that weekend.

Plans that would get me through the next few days.

I parked, got out of my car, and grabbed my bag from the trunk, headed for the bus that would take me and the guys to the airport.

But I stopped before I got on, seeing Raph getting out of his car.

My mouth opened, quickly slammed shut when I saw what my friend looked like.

Hell.

He looked like hell.

Long strides brought me to Raph's side by the time my teammate was retrieving his bag from the back seat. As he straightened, the bag tossed over his shoulder, I asked, "What's wrong?"

Dark circles under Raph's eyes. Stubble dotting his cheeks when he always shaved, only growing his beard for No Shave November, a stupid team tradition all the guys participated in. Skin pale. Hair a mess. Suit wrinkled and smelling like he'd been bathing in whiskey.

Raph's shoulders lifted and fell on a sigh. "Figured I'd at least have five fucking minutes before you got in my face, asshole."

I'd take asshole in this.

I'd own it if that meant Raph unloaded whatever in the fuck was putting this look on his face.

"You looking like that"—a wave of my hand—"you don't even have five fucking *seconds.*"

Another sigh then Raph shoved a hand in his pocket, yanked out...a crumpled piece of paper.

No.

It was glossy.

Like...photo paper.

Like...one of the ultrasound pictures that Raph had been showing off in the locker room since he'd found out he was going to be a dad, just a few days ago.

"I was supposed to go with her to the doctor. She'd kept scheduling appointments when I couldn't make it, saying there just weren't a lot of open times." A muscle in his jaw twitched. "I said I'd call the doctor, explain the situation, see if I could get to a couple of them. I wanted to hear the heartbeat and I had questions, wanted to make sure I was supporting Monica and—"

My stomach began churning.

Shit.

Had he lost the baby?

"She called when I was visiting my dad at the home"—he'd grown up with a single father who'd had a stroke a couple of months back and was currently residing in an assisted living facility—"said that they moved her appointment up, and I left right away, tried to get there in time." Another rise and fall of those big shoulders. "But I was too far away. Got there just as she was walking out. Supposedly had just finished."

Supposed—

"I'd never looked at these closely before, not the writing anyway." He shoved the picture at me, jabbed a finger at the small white letters at the top of the print-out. "I looked at the head, the legs, the heart. But not the writing...and it's not even the same hospital. Not the same date. The same fucking year, even. The— *She*—" He shoved a hand through his hair, paced away.

I was trying to make sense of that, of the fact that, yeah, the ultrasound's date that was printed on the picture was from four years before, when Raph spun back around, jabbed out his fist.

Not at me.

But at the car.

It *thunked* against the metal hard enough that I knew it had to fucking hurt.

Raph wasn't feeling anything, though. He didn't even shake out his fist when he twisted back to me and said, eyes full of fury and agony. "She was never pregnant."

I blinked, mouth dropping open.

"She made the whole damned thing up."

TWENTY-EIGHT

Kailey

SMITTY HAD CALLED me when he'd gotten to the hotel, told me about Raph, and...I'd wanted to go to him, to be there as he struggled to find a way to help his friend.

Hell, I wanted to go to *Raph* and give him a big hug.

How...

How Monica could do such a thing, could hurt Raph in that way, live that lie...

It was all kinds of fucked up that I couldn't begin to process.

A baby...was something innocent and fragile and not a joke, not a scam.

Not a *lie*.

But Smitty had it covered.

He, Theo, Cas, and Marcel had taken Raph out.

Gotten him liquored up, the venom out, and put him to bed, Smitty staying in his room to make sure he stayed asleep and hadn't done anything stupid.

He was ready to play, though, from what Smitty had told me.

"Ready to fight and hit and be a mean son of a bitch" were Smitty's exact words, and I felt more than a little scared for their opponent that night.

Raph was bound to take someone's head off.

I'd thought about going up there, something driving me to be with them—maybe it was Raph's pranks that regularly had the team in peals of laughter and usually left the person on the receiving end of them grinning. Or maybe it was the mischief-filled smiles he directed toward me in the hall, the way he'd taken to poking his head in occasionally since the ice had broken between us, asking me about my "dragon babies" from my game. Or perhaps it was the dog harness I'd found on Herman, embroidered with his name, just a few days before.

But it was mostly...I felt like part of the family

And I hated that he was hurting.

Hated that someone would do that to him.

Unfortunately, the only thing I could do at the moment was pop into his house, to make sure Monica had remained gone and to retrieve his plant.

The last I'd taken upon myself.

A stupid, silly thing to do, but also one that I was going to do anyway.

Me and Tawny were going to be good friends until Raph was ready to take her back.

Now, however, Tawny had been fertilized and watered, had been set in a nice sunny window, and I needed to go to my meeting with Marcel's dad.

I had the skeleton of what Leo had asked for, and then a slightly modified version of the website he'd asked me to create, tweaking some items I thought would provide a better user experience, some simple design things I preferred to do if I was the one doing the creating. However, because this was my first presentation and meeting with him since I'd taken the project on, I anticipated that there would be a long list of issues to address.

The functionality was there.

But clients often had *thoughts*.

And usually that meant more work for me—and often workarounds.

That was this job, however, and I couldn't complain.

Plus, these little projects, being able to use my skills in ways that I didn't always get to day-to-day, meant finding fulfillment in something that wasn't just work.

Okay, well it *was* work, but it wasn't and...

Right.

Now I actually needed to go into the restaurant where I was meeting Leo.

Pushing through the door, I spotted him at a booth in the back and felt the nerves kick up.

Words were hard, but by the time I sat down and pulled out my computer, Leo was already peppering me with questions. Which meant that I was talking about stuff in my wheelhouse, and that meant the words didn't stopper up. They came and came freely, even through the ordering and when things drifted to small talk. Did they still come easier when I was talking about the project? Definitely.

But were they getting easier because I'd found a group of people that weren't like my family, weren't like the people I'd grown up with?

Fuck yes.

And even better? Leo loved the project.

He had no major complaints, just a few minor tweaks (none of which would require major workarounds) and wanted to sit with what I'd come up with for a few days. To play with it and have Cathy, his wife, who was not a tech hound, do the same.

All of that worked for me.

But truthfully, I was having a hard time focusing on work—shocking, I knew. However, there was a TV on behind Leo, and it was showing the Breakers game and—

My eyes kept flicking to the screen.

Not that Leo wasn't watching, too.

His son was playing, but I was having a hard time focusing on anything else.

Because Smitty was on TV, and Raph was struggling—in the box (look at me go with the hockey terms! Some of the lessons Smitty had given me had actually stuck) more than out of it before the coach seemed to have decided to keep him on the bench more and on the ice less.

But even more than Raph—and my worry for his mental state—I couldn't take my eyes off Smitty.

He was big and strong and *fast*.

So damned impressive, when I was like Bambi on the ice, legs going in each direction. Smitty made it seem natural and smooth and—

Impressive.

"Marcel mentioned that you were seeing Conner."

My eyes flicked back to Leo, guilt weaving through me. "Sorry," I said. "That was unprofessional. I just..."

"...Am in love?" he asked easily, turning his chair so that it was directed toward the TV.

I blushed.

"Yeah, sweetheart," he said. "It's written all over your face." He grinned. "That's okay. I'm totally in love with my Cathy. We flew out for her work conference in town, and I've spent two days twiddling my thumbs, moaning about being apart"—he'd mentioned earlier that his wife was busy networking—"and I *miss* her." His mouth quirked. "Pathetic, huh?"

"How long have you been married?"

A fond expression. "Thirty-seven years," he said. "And I still love her more today than yesterday. Conner is a good man. I'm glad he found a nice girl."

An easy compliment.

Given without strings, without an underlying barb.

So different than my father, who never gave a compliment that wasn't underhanded.

"Thanks," I whispered. Then offered, for a reason I didn't quite process, except that, perhaps, I'd been thinking so much about him since he'd left that it was impossible to *not* offer it. "He actually asked if I'd go on the trip since it's short and falls mostly over the weekend."

Leo tilted his head to the side. "Why didn't you go?"

"Well, we had the meeting..." I trailed off when his brows went up. "What?"

"You didn't go with him because of me?"

"The project," I began, but he set his hand lightly onto mine. "Forgive me if I overstep, but in the future, please tell me to go pound sand if a side project of mine that you've been nice enough to take on stops you from spending time with the man you love."

"But you paid me."

A squeeze of my hand. "And I'm telling you that your happiness is more important than my project. You want to put me off because you and Conner can't leave your Love Den"—I bit back a laugh—"then put me off."

"I don't think that—"

He dropped his hand. "I found love, and I know what a precious gift that is. You don't waste it or put it off because of work. You grab on to it, you hold it tight, you keep it safe." His lips twitched. "Even if that means telling me you need to reschedule."

It was unprofessional.

I knew that.

But what he was saying resonated with me deeply.

Love was too precious a gift to waste.

Not for a paycheck. Not because of worry or anxiety or fearing that I'd look bad.

It was *precious*.

"Right," I whispered and reached for my wallet. "I think that means I'd better go book a flight."

Leo's expression turned appreciative, but he stayed me when I went to put some cash on the table. "I got this." A nod to the door. "And I think it does."

Heart pounding because I was *doing* this—hopping on a plane, surprising Smitty, being more impulsive than I'd ever been in my life—I got up from the table and hit the door, hustled to my car.

And by the time I'd reached the airport, my phone chimed with a text.

From Leo.

With a confirmation number for the flight he'd booked me.

TWENTY-NINE

Smitty

MY THIGHS BURNED.

My wrist stung like hell from a slash I'd taken from an asshole during the game.

Always, *always*, they managed to hit me right between where the padding on my glove ended and where my elbow pad began.

More bruises.

Bruises that were piling up now that the season was fully underway.

We'd lost three in a row, which really fucking sucked, especially when we were on the road and hearing the cheers of the hometown crowds going wild as they rooted for their team.

Especially when Brandon's words stuck in my head, mostly choosing to repeat themselves right after I'd fucked up a play or hadn't protected Martin so our goalie had let in a goal, and always, *always*, right after a loss.

I'd stolen someone's spot.

I was a fraud, a disappointment.

I didn't deserve to be there.

I—

The bus pulled into the lobby of the hotel, and I saw that there were a few women gathered, having already waited however long for the bus to show and for their chance at banging a professional hockey player, even though the team had flown in after the game over in Boston, so that meant it was nearing three in the morning.

We would have a light skate in the afternoon, and then the game that evening, so there was plenty of time to nail that player.

And I knew that quite a few of the single guys would be partaking of the offerings.

I, in the meantime, would be making sure Raph made it safely to his room then would be going the fuck to sleep, and hoping that hearing Brandon's voice would stop.

Maybe I'd text Kailey, see if she was awake.

She made the voice stop.

She—

The lights flashed on, and I grabbed my bag, slinging it over my shoulder as I waited for the guys to unload ahead of me.

Then I hopped down the stairs, ignored the cluster of women, snagging my and Raph's keys from the intern whose job it currently was to check us in and distribute them. "Still next door," she murmured, her gaze going from mine to where Raph was standing a few feet ahead of me.

"Thanks, Claire," I said, finding a smile for the timid blond, who ducked her head.

Normally, I'd tug at the end of her ponytail, would see if I could snag a smile back, find a way to get her to breathe a bit easier (what could I say, I was a sucker for the quiet ones). But today, I just didn't have it in me.

I left the thanks as it was, shoved myself next to Raph, and made sure my friend didn't do something stupid, like pick up one of the puck bunnies in the lobby. Short dresses, lots of makeup, long blond ponytails.

Always the same.

Almost like fucking plastic Barbie dolls.

But then again, most of the guys liked that plastic doll type.

I just had a thing for curvy brunettes with gorgeous emerald eyes.

Jabbing the button thankfully brought the elevator quickly, the silver doors sliding open, but just as they were closing again, a hand caught the steel panel.

A big man with a square-shaped head and an ill-fitting black suit peered inside, his eyes catching mine. "Conner Smith," he said. "I need you to come with me."

Considering he looked and sounded like law enforcement, that got me more than a few sideways looks from the guys.

"Who's asking?"

This was from Raph.

Two of the few words Raph had given this entire trip—after he'd let them *all* go during that first night of whiskey and raging and...hurt.

My friend was so fucking hurt that the pulsing radiation of it made my teeth ache anytime I was near Raph.

But he'd snapped out of it for me.

And fuck, after the voice in my head all night, that hung heavy on my heart.

"Mr. Henderson would like a word."

Mr. Henderson.

Alec Henderson.

Kailey's dad and the asshole who'd screamed at her in the hallway outside her apartment. Considering my mood and the past few nights, the last fucking thing that I wanted to be doing at that moment was to speak with the prick who'd hurt his daughter, made her have to fight to do all the things she wanted because she was so fucking terrified of the bastard that she physically shut down.

But I did have a few things that I needed to set straight with the man.

And I wouldn't put it past him to find his way to the team's floor, to start banging on doors—which was so *not* the banging that most of the guys wanted to deal with.

So, I said, "I'll drop off my stuff, meet him in the bar in ten minutes."

That made Shitty Suit's eyes narrow.

But I just shrugged my shoulders, added, "He wants to meet with me, he can wait." A shrug. "Otherwise, he can schedule time with my assistant."

A long pause.

Then the elevator alarm sounded, and Shitty Suit replied, "I'll inform Mr. Henderson."

The panels closed; the car rose. "Mr. Henderson?" Theo asked quietly.

"Kailey's asshole of a father."

The air in the elevator tightened. "What'd he do to her?" Marcel asked quietly, and the soft volume didn't mean it was any less deadly.

"Shitty father. Emotionally abusive." My teeth clinked together. "But nothing physical."

"That's just as bad," Marcel said.

Yeah. It was.

But I didn't have time to get into it with them.

I needed to drop off my shit, deal with Mr. Alec Fucking Henderson, and depending on how it went, I might have to wake Kailey up, warn her that her father was on the warpath.

"It's Kailey's story to tell," I said. "But it's not a great one, and having to deal with this bastard now, without warning, at this time of night, tells you enough about how considerate he was of his daughter over the years."

My cell buzzed, and I started to pull it from my pocket, but then the elevator doors dinged and opened, and then I wanted to find my room, get the confrontation—and I had no qualms that the coming interaction with Alec was going to be anything but a confrontation—over with. Plus, I needed to make sure Raph was in his room, wouldn't be going out and doing something stupid.

Not that he had.

But I was half-convinced it was because I'd bribed Claire with a new Breakers jersey to put us next to each other.

I was a light sleeper.

I'd hear any shenanigans.

We walked down the hall, peeling off for our rooms until I was swiping my card, watching Raph go into his before I actually opened the door.

"I got him," Theo murmured as Raph's door shut. "You do what you need to do."

"Thanks, man."

Theo went inside.

I pushed open my door and—

"Oof!"

A body collided with mine.

THIRTY

Kailey

I DIDN'T REALIZE until I was in Smitty's arms, and he was spinning me, pinning me against the door roughly enough that all my breath was squeezed out of my lungs that I should have announced myself.

"Kailey?" he exclaimed, quickly releasing the pressure he'd put on my body.

He pulled me away from the door.

"Shit, little bird," he began, running his hands over me, starting at my head. "Did I hurt you? Fuck"—he spun me around again, stroked over my shoulders, my back, my butt and legs. He even checked my ankles—"shit. I hurt you, didn't I?"

His voice broke, and my heart squeezed tight.

"Baby," I said. "*Baby*." I grabbed his hands, stilling him when he began investigating me from the front. "I'm okay."

He started to pull away from me. "I—" A shake of his head. "I'm so sorry. I—"

"Smitty. *Stop*."

He stopped.

"Breathe."

He breathed.

"Good," I said, cupping his cheeks, his beard tickling my palms. "Now, I'm guessing that you didn't get my text?"

A shake of his head. "No, little bird," he said. "I'm—"

"Stop apologizing and kiss me."

Gentle brown eyes, conflict and worry and...something else...written into the lines of his face.

"Smitty," I ordered. "Take me back into your arms and kiss me."

Thankfully, that unstuck him enough that he did.

And when he pulled back, some of the worry had faded. "You're really okay?"

I nodded. "I'm really okay, and I've made a mental note to announce myself before jumping you in the future."

His mouth quirked, just on one side. "I like it when you jump me."

"Yeah?" I felt a curl of embarrassment creep in. "Is it...I mean...is it okay that I'm here?"

A tremor went through his body, his chest hitching against mine. Then laughter bubbled up and over, filling the air, coating my skin. "Is it okay?" His arms wound tighter around me. "Little bird, when have I ever given you the impression that I don't want you to be here with me?"

I bit my lip. "I...I guess never?"

He kissed the tip of my nose, tugged my lip free of my teeth. "*Never* is right, honey." He nudged me back so we weren't standing in the hallway any longer. "Come on in and sit down, little bird, and tell me why you thought it was a good idea to be traveling in the middle of the night. How'd you get in, anyway?"

"Claire and I—"

"Hell, never mind, tell me why in the morning," he said, drawing me close again, but just as he hit my chest, he rolled so that he was on his back. "It's late. I'm tired, and I want to fuck you before we both pass out."

I grinned.

I was exhausted, knew that he had to be with the back-to-back travel, the games and practice and knowing that he had a few more games, including one that would require him to fly out to St. Louis for the next game. Then Minnesota. Then Dallas. All of which had to happen before he was going to be able to head home and we'd have our weekend together.

But I was up to being fucked.

Really ready for it.

The worst part of having a professional hockey player boyfriend was having him not be home when I was horny.

So, getting fucked then passing out in his arms sounded *real* good.

"I take it that you agree," he said, reaching for the hem of my sweatshirt and tugging it over my head. My T-shirt was gone a second after that. His lips hit mine just as he reached around behind me and began unclasping my bra when there was a pounding at the door.

The response in Smitty was instantaneous.

He went ramrod stiff, tore his mouth from mine. "Fuck," he said. "*Fuck.*"

"What is it?"

His hand came to my face, and he cupped my cheek. "I'm sorry," he whispered. "Fuck, I'm sorry."

For a second, my heart squeezed. Had I interrupted something—some*one*—coming over? Was there a woman outside that door and he'd been—

No.

Not Smitty.

And anyway, the pounding sounded familiar.

Instead of squeezing, my heart *sank.*

"Baby?" I asked.

His eyes slid closed and then opened back up, regret in their depths. "I forgot," he said. "I was supposed to go back down, and then you were here, and…" His voice dropped. "I forgot."

My body trembled. "My father."

Not a question.

Only a sigh.

Then a nod. "I'm so sorry, little bird. I—"

Something inside me snapped.

Just…snapped.

I pushed Smitty off me, grabbed my shirt from where it had landed on the carpet, then tugged it over my head and marched to the door.

I'd had enough.

More than fucking enough of this man barreling his way into my life and—

Fuck. Him.

Fuck the cold, inconsiderate bastard right up the…the… *nose.*

Yup.

Right.

Up.

The—

I whipped the door open.

The shocked expression on my father's face was almost enough to make me laugh.

Almost.

But I was too pissed to actually be amused.

Too pissed for the words to be stoppered up in my throat, to be stuck and not come out, for my father to use my struggle and my silence like a weapon, to wield it like a sword and strike me down. Too pissed to stand by and be quiet.

I'd found my voice.

And I wasn't going to let my father take it away.

"What the fuck are you doing?" I snapped, stepping forward—and yeah, I wasn't proud of it, but I stepped forward and shoved my father, hard enough that he slid back a step. "You're showing up at three in the morning at my boyfriend's hotel room—"

"He didn't come down. He said—"

The door across the hall opened, same as the ones on either side of Smitty's room, and Theo emerged, along with Raph and Marcel, concern on their faces, and at my back?

My man.

Warm and strong, his hand dropping to my waist, tugging me back against his chest.

Silent support.

Unwavering support.

And then, barely another moment passed before the guys—*my* guys because I was part of them, part of the team now—closed ranks, standing between me and my father, me and Smitty and Hank, his bodyguard.

A vein in my father's forehead pulsed, and he opened his mouth—

"I don't give a fuck that he didn't come down," I snapped. "This is his hotel, a place you didn't have permission to come barge in on. He's tired"—I swept a hand around the hall—"*all* the guys are tired, and here you are, making a scene again. And for what reason?" I asked. "To interject yourself into my life for your ten minutes a week? To pretend like you actually give a damn about me when you couldn't have given two shits my entire life?"

He opened his mouth.

But I didn't let him get anything out.

This was my turn.

Not *his*.

"But because I took this job and it wasn't your idea, because I love a man you don't know and didn't pick." I jabbed a finger in his direction. "Because I'm living my life, finally living it without your opinions or interference, you think that you have the right to show up in the middle of the night and verbally assault my boyfriend?" Smitty's arm tightened around me, and I realized I was almost leaning forward, like I was going to launch myself at my father and scratch his eyes out.

Which, I had to face, wasn't out of the realm of possibility.

Especially when my gaze drifted down, and I saw the manila envelope.

"And please tell me that's not what I think it is."

Smitty's fingers expanded on my rib cage, flexing slightly as I straightened, glaring up at my father.

"What, little bird?" he murmured.

I didn't take my eyes off my father *or* the envelope. "Either a proposal to pay you off to leave me alone," I murmured back, "or a prenup that will make you sign your life away if we ever break up."

"No amount of money could make me leave you," he murmured. "And I'd be happy to sign a prenup."

God, I loved this man.

"Not the point," I whispered, cupping his cheek.

His mouth tipped up. "I know." A beat. "But I'm stalling because..."

The elevator doors opened, and a pair of security guards stepped off.

"...Marcel called security."

My eyes shot to the other man, who knew something about

scary invaders shoving themselves into lives, who *I* knew didn't mess around. Because it had almost lost him Pru.

"Thanks," I mouthed.

A nod from the handsome forward.

"I'm just trying to do what's best for you," my father said, voice growing in volume as the guards closed in.

Doing what was best? That was...unfathomable. Because *when* had he ever done that? When he'd told me that if I only tried harder, my anxiety would go away? Or maybe to stop having a panic attack because it was inconvenient to his schedule and the charity event he wanted to attend? Or how about when I'd wanted more therapy or had asked to not perform at a piano recital or—

A hundred other things.

Big and small.

But never, *never* showing courtesy for my thoughts, my feelings, my emotions.

But...it was late, and I was tired, and I was seriously done with this night.

I wanted bed.

I wanted fucking.

I wanted—

"Did you hear me?" he snapped.

My head jerked up, the thoughts that had been weaving together in my mind scattering, a pulse of anger shooting forward. "You want to do what's best for me," I said coldly.

"Yes," he said. "Of course, I—"

"Then leave," I said, and it wasn't kind. "Leave me to my life and don't come back. Leave and stop *hurting* me over and over again. Stop making me feel like a failure and broken. Leave and make it a fucking habit for the rest of *your* life to not fucking barge in on people's lives, especially in the middle of the freaking night. Just leave and go home."

I spun in Smitty's arms, nodded to our room. "Let's all go to bed."

"Kailey."

Unfortunately, my head spun back, locking eyes with my father. The security guards had closed in, were shepherding him toward the elevator.

"I'm—"

I put my hand up. "And *I'm* not interested in what you have to say. Not at three in the morning, not accompanied by you trying to bully your way into my life, into my boyfriend's life, into these men's lives—all of whom had shown more care in knowing me *months* than you've shown me in years. So, yeah, I'm not interested in you trying to make me feel bad so that you can feel big and important." I sighed, shook my head, dropping my arm back to my side. "I think...*no.* I *know* that I'm not inter-ested in you and what you bring into my life. Not any longer. Not when you're...*this.*"

I turned back to the guys. "I'm sorry, guys," I said. "I know you're probably tired, so why don't you all just head to bed—"

"I know about you, son," my dad said, tossing the envelope of papers onto the floor. The security guards reacted quickly, one grabbing him and dragging him back to the elevator, the other nodding at Hank, who got onto the car without argument.

He might be big, but Hank was a smart one. Always had been.

"And let me be frank here," my father yelled, "you're not good enough for my daughter! Not *nearly* good enough. A man who barely passed high school? Who doesn't have a college degree? With *my* daughter, who got into—"

"Bed," I said, grabbing his face and turning it toward me. "No more," I whispered. "He's not in my—in *our* lives. Not any longer, baby. Not any longer."

Stark emotion in his eyes.

His shoulders tensing.

I heard the guys mumble their goodbyes and I managed some whispered, "Thanks" and "Goodnight," but I couldn't pull my gaze from Smitty's.

Not when he was staring at me, emotions swirling.

Then he pushed the door behind him back with his heel, tugged me inside.

The door slammed.

His arms came around me again.

And...his mouth hit mine.

THIRTY-ONE

Smitty

MY LIPS PARTED HERS, my tongue sliding inside as I scooped her up in my arms and carried her to the bed, dumping her on it in a way that wasn't the most graceful.

But I was in a hurry.

Pants off.

Shirt over her head.

Bra straps sliding down her arms. Thankfully, I'd unsnapped it earlier, so it only took a second before she was naked and beneath me.

"I am *so* fucking proud of you," I whispered, pressing my mouth to hers, to her throat, her shoulder, between her breasts. I could feel her heart pounding beneath my lips when I kissed the spot just above it, a rapid thrum-thrum that had less to do with my skills and more to do with the fact that she just kicked ass in the hallway.

Not for one moment did she appear weak.

Not for one moment did I think I would need to step in.

Did I want to?

Fuck, yeah. I wanted to plant my fist in the asshole's face.

But...that had been Kailey's fight, and she'd fucking killed it. I needed to buy Marcel a beer, thank him for interpreting his nonverbal command to call security, and the same went for the other guys. Beers all around, and maybe I'd roast some pork, make it a dinner, thank them—

Kailey shifted.

And I realized that my mouth was a couple of inches from one pouty nipple.

I could plan his grocery list later.

"I think I did good," she whispered, arching up as I kissed my way closer to that nipple.

"You did fucking fantastic, little bird."

Her eyes connected with mine and her smile sent my heart pounding even faster than it already was. "I love you," she said, leaning up slightly and planting my face between her breasts, which, really, was a pretty fucking perfect place to exist. "You know that, right?"

A nod.

A shift of my body so that I could kiss her.

"I know, little bird."

"You made me—"

"No." I rolled to my back, bringing her with me. "No, honey. *That* was you. That was my little bird, flying from the fucking nest, finding the strength, the bravery to spread her wings and soar."

She stilled.

"That's—" A shake of her head. "That's how you see me?" she asked. "That's why—?" Her eyes filled with tears. "That's why you call me that?"

I wiped a tear away. "Because I knew you'd soar, baby. I knew you would find the moment to leap, and you'd fucking *soar*."

She inhaled sharply, and there were more tears that I had to wipe away.

"Shit, Smitty," she snapped after a minute.

"What?"

I'd brought her close, was cradling her against my chest.

"Why are you so fucking perfect?" She pushed up. "Perfect for *me*. So much more than anything I could have ever dreamed of. You...you give my fantasies *life* and I love you," she whispered, fingers weaving into my beard, pressing to my jaw. "You're *perfect*."

"*Fuck*."

She blinked. "What?"

The words had struck me. Hard. Sinking in through my skin, swimming around through my bloodstream, dropping into my heart with an impact that made it nearly impossible for me to breathe, to speak. "Now you're going to be wiping away *my* tears," I murmured, covering her hand with my own.

Kailey smiled, and it sent another impact to my heart.

She leaned in, kissed lightly beneath one eye and then the other, and I knew that she was kissing away moisture, a couple of salted drops that had escaped.

But...she thought I was perfect.

Perfect for *her*.

And...I'd never had those words before, had never realized quite how much I'd needed them. Perfect. *I* was perfect. And perfect for *her*.

That was...

A lot. Everything. Too much. Not enough. Just *right*.

That feeling of *right* sank into me, holding me tight, driving me to stop fucking thinking and to flip us over, rolling to my back, wanting to show her exactly how right I could be, how perfect we could be together, how much I loved this woman who I'd wanted to watch soar through the sky and how by her doing so meant that I could fly, too.

I could let go of the dead weight and fucking soar.

Not good enough.

Not strong enough.

Not smart enough.

A disappointment. A failure. An example of mediocrity.

If I hadn't thought that, if those thoughts weren't burned into my very soul, I would have been able to shake that off, to not be bothered by the bullshit.

That the words had stuck so deep, struck so hard...

Later.

Now I had the woman I loved in my bed, and I needed to fuck her, to hold her, to make sure she knew how much she meant to me.

Later, I'd process.

Right now?

I drew her up my chest, brought that delicious pussy of hers right up onto my mouth, hands clamping down so she couldn't escape, lips and teeth and tongue working until she was grinding against me, my name a curse and a benediction as it left her mouth. I didn't stop until she was shattering, until I rolled us both over and slid inside.

Then I went slower, showing her how much she meant, how much those *words* meant.

And later, after we'd both shattered and I'd gotten us cleaned up, I brought her close, held her tight, and I lived a dream I'd always wanted, but never thought I could have.

My alarm killed me.

Fucking killed me.

But we had a skate to get to and a game that night, so I needed to head downstairs and eat.

I'd let Kailey sleep, would bring her something up when I'd finished.

Quietly slipping from her arms, I turned off the alarm, quickly dressed, and slipped from the room. Five minutes later, I had a plate full of sustenance and was heading for a table.

"Smitty."

I turned.

Saw Hazel.

And frowned.

Because she hadn't been on the trip.

"Is everything okay?"

"Sit."

A command, and Hazel wasn't the type who often gave commands. She was soft and easy and usually worked on the guys with sneaky and underhanded techniques—helping us without us actually knowing we were being helped.

So, the command had me sitting.

"Everything's fine," she said. "My mom and dad decided they wanted the perks of dating a daughter who works for a hockey team." Her face softened. "I hooked them up with tickets for tonight even though they commandeered my son and husband for sight-seeing duties."

"I...right," I murmured.

"Now"—the command was back, and I found myself sitting up straighter—"I need to talk to you."

"What's up?" I asked, shoving a piece of melon into my mouth.

Her brows lifted. "Why don't you tell me?"

Churning in my stomach, and I went to make a joke, as I always did, but then her hand covered mine. "Don't," she said.

"You're too late," I told her, unable to not make at least a *small* joke. "Kailey already smacked me around with her pretty words last night."

Hazel's head tilted to the side.

"I get why you gave me the personality tests," I said. "I even read them," I added, in case she thought I hadn't done the work she'd asked of me.

"Of that I have no doubt." She squeezed my hand, pulled back and picked up her own glass of orange juice. "You always work hard, Smitty. So why do you think that I would think any different? Is it because you think the only value you bring to the team is killing yourself to prove that you're valuable? To prove you're not a disappointment?"

That struck.

Nearly as hard as Kailey's words.

No, I didn't think that.

Except...

"I gave you those tests, not because I believe every word, or thought you would—though I think some positives can be gleaned from them," she said. "But because even though they were difficult for you to read"—a look that told me she knew about my dyslexia—"it was a challenge you would be able to overcome. A small one, with something that was difficult. Just like you've overcome the big ones."

"Right," I whispered.

"So why, just when I saw you settle down on the ice, not throwing your body around like it was invaluable, killing yourself to get the puck—"

"What? Am I not supposed to play hard?" I muttered, not liking that she was pulling back the paper that I'd managed to patch over the cracks inside me last night, destroying the work I'd put in with a few words.

"You know that's not what I mean."

I sighed.

Unfortunately, I did.

Because even with Kailey's words, there was still a part of me that thought of myself as a disappointment, would remember the sharp words, would store them somewhere deep inside. Maybe Kailey would give me that sentiment again— *No.* She *would* tell me she loved me, that I was hers, just like I'd do the same.

But unless I dealt with them, the words would always be in the wings, waiting.

"Fuck," I muttered. "Yeah, I do."

"Good," she said, her eyes gentling. "So, you'll talk to me about this stuff? We'll work on it? You'll be the open book you pretend to be so that you can live your big, bold, ballsy life?"

That had my lips quirking.

But before I could agree—and toss her a joke...because that was what I did—the elevator doors dinged, and we both looked over. Kailey stepped off the car, her hair a mess, her eyes a bit sleepy. Then...she smiled.

And fuck if I didn't feel one of the cracks inside me heal up.

"I don't have to pretend anymore," I whispered.

"No," Hazel said softly.

I shifted, managed to get my gaze off Kailey's, just for a moment, in order to meet Hazel's gentle brown eyes. "But I can't rely on just her to fill me up either."

Kailey waved.

We waved back.

"No," Hazel said. "You can't."

I took a breath, released it slowly. "I still think this point could have been more easily made by letting me break shit at a wreck room."

She grinned. "But, don't you see, Smitty? Your superpower isn't hitting stuff so hard until it shatters—"

Kailey was almost to our table.

"It's putting things back together again."

EPILOGUE

Kailey

I GRINNED as I peeked into the small bag that currently held my Christmas present for Smitty's parents.

It wasn't much—just a pair of earrings I'd thought the cool and hip Celeste would like, and a bottle of whiskey that was Ryan's favorite.

I'd gotten lucky that I'd been able to pick up the gifts, considering it was Christmas Eve and the shops had been packed, and his parents hadn't originally been planning on coming to visit and celebrate the holiday until after the New Year.

But their cruise to Hawaii had gotten canceled, and for some reason they'd decided to freeze their butts off in Baltimore instead of finding another way to the tropics.

I would be glad to see them.

They'd visited a few more times since that initial—dramatic —dinner, and things had been smooth and fun, and Smitty had been able to talk to them a bit about all the things that had been going through his head.

That had brought clarity and understanding, and...tears from Celeste.

But she'd recouped quickly, had held her big, broad son in her arms, and they all had talked for a long time.

Slowly, I was watching Smitty shed that hidden burden, the buried pain he'd carried for far too long, the one masked by jokes and a big personality.

I was watching *him* soar.

My lips turned up further as I set the bag beneath the tree at Smitty's place—a house that was going to become mine soon. My lease was up in May, but we'd decided to break it, and I was going to move my stuff in over the All-Star break.

Though, it may be less of a break and more of me frantically getting my stuff in so that I could watch Smitty take part in the festivities.

He'd been playing...incredible.

The rosters weren't publicly announced yet, but everyone knew he'd be on the roster.

Because he was flying, those heavy weights released.

Only...there was one more weight that still remained.

So hopefully, my luck—the one that had turned up pretty earrings, a bottle of whiskey, and the wallet (boring but I'd been desperate, okay) I'd tucked into the bag behind the tree—would hold.

Because...I'd done something.

Something that might backfire, especially considering it was definitely overstepping boundaries.

But...

I loved Smitty.

I wanted him to be happy.

I wanted them *all* to be happy.

So, when I'd heard that his parents hadn't spoken to Brandon since the night at CeCe's, except for the occasional check-in to make sure he was breathing, I'd known I had to do something.

Even *I* had found a way forward with my dad.

He'd given me radio silence for a month, then had called, and…I didn't know why, maybe old habit, maybe stupidity, maybe…just not quite knowing what he wanted and had been overcome with curiosity to find out.

I'd picked up the call.

And…he'd been tentative, the first thing off his tongue, an apology.

That didn't erase everything. Hell, who was I kidding? It didn't erase *anything*. I'd suffered for years because of his actions. But…also…

I could have a polite conversation with him for ten minutes once a week.

Maybe over time it would become something else.

Right now, that was the extent that I was able to allow.

And I considered it a win. A *big* win. That I could set and keep that boundary, that he wasn't cruel and demanding and… flying out on a fucking plane in the middle of the night.

Would I ever forgive him? No. I didn't think I had that in me.

But I might find some way forward that wasn't a burden on me.

And that would be enough.

So right.

Hopefully, Smitty would understand that was why I'd called his brother. I wanted them happy and to find a way forward and—

Brandon had been out of line.

But Brandon…

He'd also been dumped by his girlfriend, fired from his job, hadn't slept in days—and hadn't divulged that to any member of his family. Carrying burdens was a Smith specialty apparently.

He hadn't wanted to ruin Smitty's night.

And he had—sort of. Because it had broken the ice for me, brought me and Smitty closer together...and now I'd given him the chance to come, own up, apologize, and find a way forward.

I'd told him that, too. During our conversation, after I'd dragged the truth out of him.

Well, *ordered* him to tell Smitty and his parents.

Though, dragging the truth out of him had been accurate.

Look at me.

Soaring and ordering.

My two new favorite adjectives.

But now that it was getting close to go time (to when Brandon would show up), the nerves were getting the better of me. Smitty was in the kitchen, finishing up cooking dinner. His parents were with him, and I could hear his mom laughingly joking to send Smitty away from the stove if he burned the gravy.

And Brandon would be here—

A knock at the front door.

"Shit," I whispered, standing up from amongst the presents and moving away from the tree. I hurried to the front door.

But...Smitty beat me there, brows pulled together as he reached for the handle.

"Baby," I began.

His gaze flicked to mine, brows drawing further when he took in what was no doubt a panicked expression on my face. "Little bird—"

The knock came again.

"Please don't hate me," I whispered, even though I knew he wouldn't.

"Why—" A shake of his head. "I could never—"

I reached him then. "I know," I said. "I'm talking crazy because I did something crazy and—" Another knock. "I hope that you won't be mad."

A breath.

I opened the door.

And Smitty went still behind me.

Brandon...looked like hell. His face was covered in stubble, he had a backpack hanging off one shoulder, a bag of presents on the other. But the stark expression on his face was worse. This was a man who was hurting.

Smitty knew it.

"I'm sorry," Brandon said, the words a rasp. "I know that doesn't change it. I had...not *reasons*," he said. "But I wasn't in my right mind, and I'm so fucking ashamed that I said those things, that I tried to sabotage your happiness just because I was a miserable bastard." His chest rose and fell. "I'll go if you want. I know I shouldn't have come, but Kailey asked and—and don't be mad at her, okay? She's just trying to help." Another breath. "I know I shouldn't be here, but this last month has been hell, and—"

Smitty *moved*.

One second, he was behind me.

The next he was gently nudging me to the side, moving forward and...

Embracing his brother.

The backpack hit the ground.

The presents followed suit.

I heard something crack inside Brandon's bag, and knew that no one was going to give a fuck. Not when Celeste and Ryan overheard the commotion and came into the hall, not when they joined the hug. Not when they moved into the living room and Brandon began sharing all the things that he hadn't shared before that dinner.

I gathered up the bags, dumped the bottle of whiskey that had shattered (luckily, in the gift bag), and then had moved into the kitchen, checking on the gravy, finishing up dinner.

Serving it up onto plates because no one wanted to leave the living room.

Brandon was still talking, still apologizing and explaining and owning up.

So, I quietly delivered plates.

But when I went to slip out again, to give them privacy, Smitty caught me around the waist with his arm, tugging me onto his lap.

"I love you," he whispered.

The small part of me that had been worried about him being mad at me relaxed. "I love you," I murmured back.

Brandon glanced up from his nearly permanent study of his hands.

The emotions in his eyes almost burned me.

But then he said, "I'm so fucking glad you have that, bro. *That's* what I should have said that night. *That's* what I'll say from every day here on out. *That's*—" His voice broke, and he glanced down at his hands again.

After a minute, Smitty's chest moved behind me. "Thanks, Brand." Then again, his deep breath rocking me forward and back gently. "Now, are we continuing with the Smith tradition of watching *Home Alone* or should we change it up and watch *Elf*?"

Celeste grinned and saluted me with her wine glass. "You know what?" The glass rose a little higher. "I think this is the year for new traditions."

LATER THAT NIGHT, just as Christmas Eve was turning into Christmas morning, as me and Smitty lay together in his bed, long after we'd gotten his parents and Brandon settled in the guest rooms, after *Elf* and *Home Alone* had been consumed, Smitty rolled to his nightstand, opened the drawer, and pulled out a box.

"I think this is the year for new traditions, too, little bird."

He opened the lid, revealing a diamond ring inside.

"I love you, Kailey Henderson," he said, gathering me close after he plucked the ring from the box and rested it on the tip of my finger. "I want to help you fly and watch you soar. I want to make babies with you and watch *Elf* every year on Christmas. I want to do all the little things that bring a smile to your face, knowing that you always do the same in return. I want us to find our happiness, forever, without the weights of our pasts. I want—"

I cupped his cheek. "I want to marry you, Smitty."

"I have more to my speech."

My lips turned up. "I have no doubt that it was about to turn dirty."

Dancing brown eyes. "How did you know?"

A shake of my head, a brush of my lips to his. "Because, more than anything else, more than anyone else, my heart has always known yours."

Then as Eve turned into morning, as the man I loved with everything inside me slid the ring down my finger, Smitty gave me the rest.

It *was* dirty.

So dirty that it led to fucking—quiet fucking, but still with our bodies coming together and my heart racing, my lungs sawing.

But it ended with me soaring, Smitty's arms around me.

And that meant it was perfect.

Thank you for reading! I hope you loved meeting Smitty and Kailey as much as I did! But Smitty's story doesn't end with the Breakers hockey team! If you want even more big, bearded hockey players who fall hard and fast for the women they love *and* get your Smitty fix, pick up book one in the Grizzlies Hockey series, MARRIED TO NUMBER TWENTY-TWO. **I signed the contract. I just didn't expect her to show up ten years later, ready to cash it in.** CLICK HERE TO READ MARRIED TO NUMBER TWENTY-TWO NOW>

Read on for a sneak peek below!

Aiden

I WAKE up to a heavy knock on my condo's front door and glare blearily at my phone in the charger.

"Two in the fucking morning," I mutter, grabbing a pillow and clamping it over my ears. "It's two o'clock in the morning on my fucking birthday, and I have to deal with this shit."

This shit being my neighbors.

It's not the first time they've pounded drunk on my door, desperate for their roommate to let them in to what they think is their apartment.

This was sort of funny the first time.

I remember those days, drinking too much, being dumb.

But after the second and the third—where I gained status

into the inner circle and a code to the keypad to their apartment door—it was no longer cute.

Now, six months later and countless times of bailing them out, I'm *so* not in the mood.

Especially when it's my fucking birthday.

The knocking cuts off and I think—*pray*—that they've gotten the hint.

But it's approximately two seconds later when it starts up again.

I glance at my phone again, see that really five minutes have passed, making it two-seventeen and officially my birthday.

Some present.

I could try to ignore it—but that just means extending the torture. Sighing, I toss back the blankets and stomp to my apartment door, whipping it open to reveal a slender brunette on my doorstep.

"Ho, mama," she says, gaze taking a slow perusal down my body.

"Who the fuck are you?"

"It's me. Luna."

I stare at her, uncomprehendingly.

"From Rockfield?" she adds.

Recognition begins to dawn. "Luna Maybelle?"

"Yup! That's me." She nods, grinning, and I see it then, the glimpse of my best friend from the childhood rink I grew up playing at come out in her smile. Mischief and life. Joy and hard work.

Summers spent spending every spare moment together— her figure skating, me playing hockey.

But she's not little Luna anymore.

Christ, she's anything but—tall, beautiful, curves for days— and she's staring at me.

Because I'm staring at her.

Fucking hell.

I spur myself into motion.

"Luna! Oh my God!" I pull her into a hug. "What the hell are you doing here?"

"It's your birthday!" She holds up a piece of paper that looks faintly familiar. "And, well, it's mine too, remember?"

That's right.

We have the same birthday.

"We're both twenty-five, single, and—"

My eyes narrow in on the paper. It's crumpled and stained, as though it's years old.

A purple and pink swirl decorates the edges and suddenly I remember her painstakingly drawing it as we sat side-by-side at one of the high top tables of the ice rink, waiting for the Zamboni to finish cutting the ice.

Her brow had been furrowed. Her movements carefully controlled.

And I had been obsessing over how pink her lips were and what her butt looked like in her skating dress, so much so that I barely remember what we'd been drawing.

No, I think hard, grabbing on to those memories, not what we'd been *drawing*.

The contract we'd put together.

The contract my hormonal twelve-year-old self had signed.

With a sparkly pink colored pencil.

A giant boulder settles in my stomach, but before I can snap myself out of the horror of those memories, she shoves the paper in my hands then throws her arms around my neck.

"We're getting married!"

· · ·

CLICK HERE TO READ MARRIED TO NUMBER TWENTY-TWO NOW>

The next book in the Breakers Hockey series is BEWITCHED. Find out what happens to Beth and Raph and the babies.
She had a secret.
One she had spent her whole life running from.
CLICK HERE TO READ BEWITCHED NOW> or read on for a sneak peek below...

Raph, One Year Later

I PUSHED MY DRINK AWAY, knowing that if I finished it, I would get sloppy.

I didn't get sloppy.

I had a careful recipe of drinking at CeCe's and consuming enough food and stopping at the right time to prevent me from getting sloppy.

Drown out the voices in my head.

But do it in a way that didn't bring any intervention from my teammates, or worse, Hazel. Sometimes the team psychologist looked at me as though she could see through the shield I'd erected.

And I couldn't have that.

I was too busy letting the hurt and betrayal eat at my very bones.

Sighing, I threw some bills on the bar top, started to push away, to go home to my empty house, with the empty rooms, the doors perpetually closed.

"Raph!"

A shiver down my spine.

Fucking hell.

Not *her*.

Anyone but *her*.

Except, even as I turned, I knew it was going to be her. Going to be...Beth.

My hands shook, fingers clenching into fists, lungs seizing.

I'd been avoiding her like the fucking plague. First, she was beautiful and loud and pushy, and I didn't want her in my business, didn't want *any* woman in my business. I'd been there, done that, got the fucking souvenir broken heart from Hurricane Monica.

Or maybe Hurricane Liar was more accurate.

She'd lied about something so fucking big that I didn't know how I was ever going to trust another woman.

Ever.

Especially one as beautiful as Beth.

Monica had been gorgeous, impeccably dressed, her makeup always done—high maintenance at its best, and maybe that made me a dick who'd deserved what was coming to me, but I'd always liked my women a little high-maintenance.

Beth was just as gorgeous, as put together, and she was a total ballbuster (something else that used to make me hard).

But I hadn't been avoiding her for those reasons.

Or not *only* those reasons.

The biggest one...the one that my eyes dropped to, was leading her charge his way.

The soft rounded curve of her belly.

Fuck.

That sliced fucking *deep*, because I hadn't seen that with Monica. Because Monica had lied about carrying my baby.

Because she'd never been pregnant at all. I hadn't seen her belly grow, hadn't felt our baby move, hadn't held my son or daughter in my arms.

How in the fuck was I grieving for a baby that hadn't existed?

But I was.

And it sliced deep, fucking killed me that Pru and Marcel were going to have two. *Two* babies that Beth was carrying for her because Pru couldn't and—

I was a fucking asshole.

Pru had been attacked, traumatically, had barely survived, and Beth was doing something wonderful by carrying Pru and Marcel's babies.

And every time I looked at her, I felt sick to my stomach.

Unfortunately, there was nowhere to escape—not without looking like a douche, anyway. I might have douchebag thoughts and be a total asshole on the inside, but I tried not to let that bleed out onto the people around me.

So...I waited for her to come near, and when she smiled and started to hop onto the stool next to me, I helped her up, ignoring the zing the contact brought to my fingertips.

It had been a year since I'd touched a woman.

A fucking year.

But...I hadn't been able to bring myself to do that.

And the feel of Beth's skin beneath my fingertips, the way it felt like silk, how she smelled—floral and fruity—how she cradled her little bump, as though protecting the babies inside her womb from the outside world...they reminded me.

Some of Monica and how she'd been.

Some of how she hadn't.

Plenty of fruit and flowers and silk. No protective cradling. No baby.

I clenched my free hand into a fist again, waited for Beth to settle.

"Thank God, you're here," Beth exclaimed. "It's not Cheese Night Extravaganza, but I'm starving and losing my mind because I *need* mozzarella sticks." She smiled, glanced down. "Okay, these babies are growing, so *they* need them, but since they're going in my mouth, *I* need them and—"

She broke off, cheeks flushing prettily.

Probably able to see how much that hurt.

Because Beth was smart—pretty and funny and loud and high maintenance and *fucking* smart.

That made her dangerous, and her next words proved it.

"Sorry," she whispered, her hand resting on my arm. "I didn't think. That was really inconsiderate." She pulled back, nibbled on her red-painted lip. Her gaze hit on the money on the bar. "I should let you go. I'll wait for a table—"

"What do you want to eat?" I asked gruffly. "Besides the mozzarella sticks," I added when she lifted her brows. "Something with at least a *bit* of nutritional value."

"Umm...nachos?" she said.

A curl of amusement in my chest.

And hell, it had been so long since I'd felt that emotion that it took me a minute to recognize what it was.

"They have vegetables on them," she added, a bit mulishly and probably because I hadn't responded, given that it had taken me a long fucking time to recognize the emotion of *amusement.*

"Salsa's not a vegetable," I said.

Her blue eyes narrowed, her long red hair twitched when she spun slightly to face me. "Peppers are. *Olives* are."

"Olives are technically fruit."

Those eyes narrowed further.

And that amusement grew.

But I didn't do anything about it, just waved down the bartender, put in an order for club soda, nachos, mozzarella sticks, and a side of fruit.

When the bartender went to plug that into the register, I turned back to Beth.

Who was staring at me with wide eyes. "You know what I drink?"

I knew a lot about her. What she drank, that if I'd ordered a salad, she wouldn't touch it, but that she would deign to eat the fruit in the name of something healthy.

But I couldn't reveal any of that, could I?

Not when I was acid inside, not when that acid was eating away at the man I was inside.

So, I just said, "I've hung out with you, Hazel, Pru, and company enough. I know what you *all* drink."

That dropped her brows, though a thoughtful expression took the place of surprise. "Right," she whispered.

They sat in silence—or rather, *I* sat in silence—as we waited for her food to come. But then her food *did* come and because I was sitting next to her, I stole a mozzarella stick with the lightning-fast reflexes of a professional hockey player and earned a glare in return for my antics.

Eventually, though, I found myself joining her in conversation, not just listening to her talk to me, to her funny quips and stories and antics, but actually talking.

Enjoying myself.

Paying for her meal before she could.

I stood, put out an arm to help her down as she was regaling me with a tale about a misbehaving coworker.

"And then—"

Her face went pale the moment her feet hit the floor.

"Beth?" I asked, reaching out with my other arm, wrapping it around her.

"What's—"

She took a step.

Her eyes rolled back.

And...she collapsed.

CLICK HERE TO READ BEWITCHED NOW>

BREAKERS HOCKEY SERIES

<u>Broken</u>
<u>Boldly</u>
<u>Breathless</u>
<u>Ballsy</u>
<u>Bewitched</u>
Blowout
Breathe
A Breakers Christmas
Blazed
Bound

Hate missing Elise's new releases? Love contests, exclusive excerpts and giveaways?
Then signup for Elise's newsletter here!

www.elisefaber.com/newsletter

And join Elise's fan group, the Fabinators (https://www.facebook.com/groups/fabinators) for insider information, sneak peaks at new releases, and fun freebies! Hope to see you there!

If you enjoy my series, considering supporting me on PATREON! Get access to early releases, bonus content, character art, audiobooks, special edition covers, swag, and much more!

CLICK HERE TO SUPPORT ME>

I so appreciate your help in spreading the word about my books, including sharing with friends! Please leave a review on your favorite book site!

Gold Hockey (**all stand alone**)

Blocked

Backhand

Boarding

Benched

Breakaway

Breakout

Checked

Coasting

Centered

Charging

Caged

Crashed

A Gold Christmas

Cycled

Caught

Cap

Covered

Crushed

Changed

Scored

Breakers Hockey (all stand alone)

Broken

Boldly

<u>Breathless</u>

<u>Ballsy</u>

<u>Bewitched</u>

Blowout

Breathe

A Breakers Christmas

Blazed

Bound

Sierra Hockey Series

Over the Line

Caught from Behind

The Big Skate

On the Fly

Rush Hockey Trilogy #1

Big Puck Energy

Filthy Puckboy

So Pucking Over It

Rush Hockey Trilogy #2

Love, Pucks, and Other Stories

All's Fair in Pucks and War

No Pucks Lost Between Us

Rush Hockey Novellas

Puck and Make Up

Eagles Hockey Series (all stand alone)

Broken Laces

Lace 'em Up

Knotted Laces

Loaded Laces

Lucky Laces

***Billionaire's Club* (all stand alone)**

Bad Night Stand

Bad Breakup

Bad Husband

Bad Hookup

Bad Divorce

Bad Fiancé

Bad Boyfriend

Bad Blind Date

Bad Wedding

Bad Engagement

Bad Bridesmaid

Bad Swipe

Bad Girlfriend

Bad Best Friend

Bad Rebound

Bad Romance

Bad Business

Bad Billionaire's Quickies

Love, Action, Camera (all stand alone)

Dotted Line

Action Shot

Close-Up

End Scene

Meet Cute

***Love After Midnight* (all stand alone)**

Rum And Notes

Virgin Daiquiri

On The Rocks

Sex On The Seats

Life Sucks Series

Train Wreck

Hot Mess

Dumpster Fire

Clusterf*@k

FUBAR

Perfect Storm

Free Fall

Lost Cause

***Roosevelt Ranch Series* (all stand alone, series complete)**

Disaster at Roosevelt Ranch

Heartbreak at Roosevelt Ranch

Collision at Roosevelt Ranch

Regret at Roosevelt Ranch

Desire at Roosevelt Ranch

***Phoenix Series* (read in order)**

Phoenix Rising

Dark Phoenix

Phoenix Freed

***Phoenix: LexTal Chronicles* (rereleasing soon, stand alone, Phoenix world)**

From Ashes

In Flames

To Smoke

***KTS Series* (all stand alone, series complete)**

Riding The Edge

Crossing The Line

Leveling The Field

Scorching The Earth

Cocky Heroes World

Tattooed Troublemaker

ABOUT THE AUTHOR

USA Today bestselling author, Elise Faber, loves chocolate, Star Wars, Harry Potter, and hockey (the order depending on the day and how well her team -- the Sharks! -- are playing). She and her husband also play as much hockey as they can squeeze into their schedules, so much so that their typical date night is spent on the ice. Elise is the mom to two exuberant boys and lives in Northern California. Connect with her in her Facebook group, the Fabinators or find more information about her books at www.elisefaber.com.

facebook.com/elisefaberauthor

amazon.com/author/elisefaber

bookbub.com/profile/elise-faber

instagram.com/elisefaber

tiktok.com/@elisefaberauthor

goodreads.com/elisefaber